I0579395

The
LEGEND
of
EYDIS

◎ ◎ ◎

Not all legends are born of lies …

C. S. Johnson

Dedicated to Sam. There are dragons to be conquered in this world, but I hope I have proved to be worthy of your efforts.

This is also for Jordan, my favorite Viking by choice, and my friend by grace.

But most of all, this is dedicated to Ryan. You not only slay the beast inside my heart, but you also tame it and bring out the beauty inside of it. Thank you for loving me as your wife for these last ten years; as long as I have you by my side, I know the best is yet to come.

Special Thanks to my (Almost) Famous Readers and Patrons!

Kelly C.
Nina P.
Pat C.

Terri R.
David W.
David S.
Donna S.
Chris S.
Natalia K.
Beth C.
Brynn S.

Jerilyn B.

Richard B.
Marty H.

My additional thanks:

Amanda W., for your kindness in *Northern Lights, Southern Stars*; Katrina P., for your encouragement, also from *Northern Lights, Southern Stars;*

Crystal M. – for your keen sight, and bigger vision; and Cathy H. – for all your editing work. My story might be good, but with your friendship and dedication, it is much better.

And finally, one last thanks goes to the Panera Bread Company—this book was made possible in large part because of all the refills I had while I worked, so you have my thanks!

For more dragons, curses, and tragic adventure,
check out C. S. Johnson's
Eydis: The Island of the Dragon Bride,
a novella adventure set before this story!

<u>1</u>

❋   ❋   ❋

Ever since his brother died, night was no longer kind to Bjorn Kyvansson.

Terror filled his mind as he slept; inside his dreams, he could see the chasm between the worlds of waking and dreaming, time and timelessness, with no absolution on either side. Scenes of suffering and despair danced in his sight, stringing familiar faces alongside foreign places. Flashes of white and green and red danced together, and agony laced between each beat of his heart as he saw his brother die under the dark shadow of a dragon.

"Brother." Bjorn jolted awake, sitting up and clutching his chest, trying to soothe his wildly beating heart. The chill in the air spoke a tangible dread that flowed from his dreams; as his breathing slowed and his heartbeat steadied, Bjorn tasted salt on his lips.

Tears or sweat? Bjorn frowned, and then he discarded the question.

Some questions were better left unanswered.

He glanced over at the turf wall separating his room from the rest of his family. From the small slips of moonlight passing through the roof thatches, Bjorn could see the faintest stream of green trails against the sky, as auroras gradually faded across the horizon. The moon rode high in the clouds, and the sun remained beyond the roof of the world for now, as it would for several hours yet. Bjorn had only slept for a few hours.

He sighed. His nightmares were nothing out of the ordinary—not after Sterlig's death.

Bjorn's harrowing dreams had come the first night after he and his family learned Sterlig was dead.

At the time, Bjorn thought that his nightmares would go away.

Several months later, he knew he had been wrong.

If anything, the dreams have gotten worse of late. He dropped his head into his hands.

"Sterlig," Bjorn murmured. In his dream, he had seen his older brother face the last moments of his life. Sterlig had struggled to survive as he fought against his enemy, but in the end, he had died, tragically and horrifically—and all alone, far from home, on foreign, enchanted soil.

When Sterlig had announced his intent to go to the island of Eydis to slay the dragon there, Bjorn was not surprised. Ever since the dragon first appeared a hundred years ago, prince and pillager alike had died trying to slay the monster, the dragon of Eydis. Killing the dragon was exactly the sort of challenge his older brother enjoyed. Even if no one had survived a fight with the great beast before.

Sterlig had dismissed Bjorn's concern.

"But what makes you think you'll succeed, when others have failed?" Bjorn had asked.

"I have a reason to win." Sterlig's strong chin jutted out with pride, and there was no hint of doubt at all on his smug, sunburnt face.

Bjorn looked over at his brother's empty pallet across from his and shook his head. He did not want to think about his brother's fate any more than he wanted to dream about it. He folded his hands together briefly and tried to say a prayer, grateful that his mother's god was a god of spirit as well as flesh, and he could trust he prayed to a being who knew what Bjorn did not know how to express—or admit.

And only God the Allfather knew there was plenty Bjorn did not want to admit when it came to his brother's death, especially when it came to—

No.

Bjorn squeezed his eyes shut, forcing himself to stop before he thought about Arja Freydottir.

He did not like to think about Sterlig, but Bjorn hated thinking about his brother's intended bride even more.

Bjorn clenched his fists. He pushed aside the blankets on his sleeping pallet and reached for one of his woolen tunics. He pulled back his shoulder-length hair, tying it back with a band. The potash soap he used to keep it clean during the summer had faded, allowing the dull, natural brown to reappear. It needed to be bleached again, soon.

Bjorn sighed and pulled on his boots, before he started toward the door.

Only to stop, as a loud *clash* interrupted him.

Bjorn froze; his back went rigid, and his breathing stopped.

Slowly, he turned around.

And there it was.

His sword laid on the floor, the blade radiating a greenish, malevolent glow.

Bjorn felt his breathing constrict even further. Many of his countrymen would say the trolls and elves hiding in the countryside had cursed him, that the gods of *Forn Sidr*, the old way, were playing with him or that Odin's night dragons wound their way across the coming winter skies and infiltrated his dreams. There were plenty of traders who would offer similar counsel, saying it was the work of the otherworldly and the supernatural. As Bjorn stared at the sword before him—the same one Sterlig had taken to Eydis, the same one that their friends, Finnar and Jon, had returned to him—it was hard to disagree.

His home, Kyvan, was only an outlying trading post in a small corner of the world, but he also knew it was a mistake to give legends more credence than they were due. His dreams were not from other creatures, nor did they have divine origins. They came from the questions which had been running ceaselessly through his mind since he learned of his brother's death.

Or so he thought.

Just as Bjorn reached out for the fallen sword, his father let out a loud groan from his bed one room over. Bjorn jerked his hand back, and the sword gleamed with ghoulish amusement. The eagle head he had designed for the pommel twinkled while his father fell back into mumbling silence.

"Thank you, almighty Father." Bjorn let out a grateful prayer of praise as he picked up his sword. If the choice lay between waking up his father and carrying a cursed sword, Bjorn was more than happy to risk the latter.

After Sterlig died, Keyvak Ragnork was only ever angry or drunk while he was awake. While it strained their family, Bjorn knew his father was grieving in his own way. Keyvak and Sterlig had bonded over the years as they hunted and sailed on Viking raids. The proudest Bjorn had ever seen his father look was when the chieftain of Kyvan had named Sterlig among his favorite soldiers and sparring partners.

But that was before Sterlig decided to go off and face the dragon of Eydis.

Bjorn ran his hand over his sword, studying it carefully. Even in its scabbard, he intimately knew every fine detail of the pommel, the hilt, everything—right down to the runic inscription on the blade. While his father and brother hunted and pillaged, Bjorn had worked with his Uncle Lodd to become a blacksmith and bladesmith. After years as his uncle's apprentice, he prepared his own sword for battle and training, pouring his heart into his work.

Naturally, Sterlig had taken the sword from him, claiming it as his own before heading off to Eydis.

Bjorn's fingers dropped from the sword as the greenish tint disappeared entirely.

The glow disappeared, but his guilt did not.

As fine as the sword was, he couldn't help but wonder if he was to blame for Sterlig's death.

Soft footsteps approached him from behind, and he tightened his grip on the hilt.

"There is nothing you could've done, Bjorn."

Elska Eliadottir's voice was gentle as it cut through the air between them, but pain struck him squarely in the heart. He did not deserve his mother's graciousness, no matter how much he knew she loved him. Elska's assurance was meant as absolution, but Bjorn found no truth or comfort in it.

"I know," he lied.

"When you speak like that, you sound just like your father," his mother replied smoothly as she brushed back her loose curls of dark hair, now streaked with gray, that trickled out of their braided knot. A small glimmer of wry amusement sparkled in her jasper eyes. "Especially after I tell him he needs to stop drinking."

"I'm nothing like Father." Bjorn cleared his throat and tried to soften his tone. "He tells me that often enough."

"All men are prone to self-destruction," Elska told him quietly. "Keyvak has mead and ale as his poison of choice, a slow-acting one that easily passes through his system, assuming he doesn't injure himself on the way home. But you're young, Bjorn—no matter if you've reached eighteen summers and you're a head taller than me. I know you well enough to know your method of personal affliction has nothing to do with the head and everything to do with the heart."

Is it possible she knows? Bjorn stiffened, briefly thinking of Arja again. He did not like the thought that his mother could guess at his secrets.

"There's no need for you to keep blaming yourself for Sterlig's death," Elska continued, allowing Bjorn to slowly breathe again. "Your father says many things and repeats them many times, but you and I know that doesn't make them true."

Despite his mood, Bjorn laughed quietly, still unwilling to wake his father with careless noise. "He seems to think that's how it works."

"Authority without truth is only imagined power." Elska came up beside Bjorn and put her hand on his shoulder. "And if you are blaming yourself for *my* grief, you may stop. The Living God has given me peace over Sterlig's death. And he can do that for you, too, my son."

Bjorn finally turned to face her, his eyes catching the twinkle of gold from the small chain around her neck. The necklace disappeared under the collar of her woolen aprondress, hiding the golden crucifix it bore. He knew from her stories growing up that it was the last gift his grandmother gave to her before she passed, and it was his mother's most prized possession.

"I'm thankful God is willing to give you peace." Bjorn kept his tone neutral, not wanting to admit how he envied his mother.

"I know Keyvak has not been easy on you," Elska murmured quietly. "Don't let him fill your mind with falsehoods."

"I can handle the falsehoods better than his debts."

The light in his mother's eyes dimmed. "If he's not careful, Keyvak is going to end up a slave."

Bjorn quickly pressed a kiss to his mother's cheek, already sorry he had said anything. It had been an act of self-defense to keep her away from his secrets, but he had caused her pain.

"There are plenty of details Father and Frey Gilsson haven't discussed," Bjorn told her. "Jon's told me that he and Finnar are in just as much trouble. Father blames them for stealing our family's knarr."

"I'm sure Sterlig was behind that. He needed a ship to get to Eydis."

"But Frey's thralls are the ones who ended up burning it." Bjorn gripped his sword uneasily. "They said it was haunted."

"What foolishness. But in regards to our family's debts, I will remain hopeful for now," Elska murmured, touching the gold chain at her throat. "No sense in worrying when there's nothing else to be done."

"Frey will give you plenty of grief if you let him. He's always been a miser."

"Arja's always said so, too."

A telling silence slipped between mother and son as Bjorn busied himself by tying the sword to his belt.

"I've missed Arja's visits." Elska gave Bjorn an amused look. "I was hoping she would still come by, but perhaps it's too painful for her yet."

"Perhaps." Bjorn's jaw tightened. "For now, we should respect her wishes."

"Have you seen her in town at all?"

Yes.

Bjorn could conjure a picture of Arja inside his mind in the blink of an eye, and he'd done it often enough there was no lack of detail in his memory. He could see her bright blonde hair styled back from her large, bright green eyes and her smooth, wintery skin. He'd seen her at least four times in the last three days as he delivered his commissions and haggled for goods in Kyvan. The last he had seen her, she was beside the perfume traders from Eydis. Her small mutt, Ulf, had been barking happily at the crowd while she talked with a large, dark man in a friendly manner.

"I haven't talked with her," Bjorn said. "If I see her when I go to town later, I will pass along your greetings and well-wishes."

"Thank you." Elska smiled. "So, you are going to town? Geira mentioned you have a good reputation for your work. Lodd would be proud."

A small lump formed in his throat at the mention of his uncle. His good humor and insightful instruction, not just in metalworking but in other areas, sustained Bjorn's spirits even on the worst days. When Lodd had succumbed to a fever two winters before, it was the first time Bjorn had felt truly alone.

"I miss him," Bjorn admitted.

"We will see him again one day," Elska whispered, her own grief evident. She patted Bjorn on the shoulder. "Until then, honor his legacy for me, will you?"

"Yes, Mother." Bjorn nodded. It was not a question of honor. Honor was a given, was sacred to their way of life in Snæland, among families and communities alike. Everyone from the chieftain of Kyvan, Jarl Vidur Thordirsson, down to the youngest farmhand had a duty to fulfill to others. Bjorn took his duties and his honor seriously. He knew firsthand how destructive the sacrilegious could be.

Bjorn walked out of the house to his forge, watching the freedom of the auroras dancing in the sky. They didn't have a place they needed to go, and they were not bound by the dictates of his home as he was. Stuck between his nightmarish dreams and his daytime concerns, Bjorn was certain of the passage of the time, but not of his purpose within it.

When he glanced down at the sword, he was not surprised to see it glowing with its eerie green aura, matching the trails of the light across the night sky. He tightened his grip on the hilt of the sword and hurried toward his forge. Despite the weakness of the firepit's flames, the air's chilliness dissipated a little. He leaned the sword that had failed to save Sterlig against the doorframe, eager to leave it behind as he lost himself in his work.

Nothing could stay close for long as he worked—not his mother's worry, his father's neglect, and not even Arja's love for Sterlig—when he was focused. His world fell into order, and it remained so, until a sharp clashing sound suddenly cut through his concentration.

Bjorn jumped at the noise behind him and glanced back. His sword had fallen over again.

Flashes of his dream ran through his mind as his steady rhythm tapered off.

Bjorn carried the sword back to his worktable and set it down, forcing himself to ignore the glow it emitted.

It had to be the auroras—or were the colors his own imaginings, born out of guilt?

Bjorn shook his head. His mother was right—there was nothing he could've done to stop Sterlig from going to Eydis. Bjorn knew his brother very well, and discouraging Sterlig from going would have only pushed his brother there faster.

There was nothing he could do now, either.

Sterlig was dead.

Bjorn could only move forward with his own life.

But the thought of moving on only made him more uneasy, and his guilt increased further as Bjorn went back to work.

He was certain God would grant him peace if he asked for it, but he knew that it wasn't peace he wanted.

He pictured Arja's face again, with her pert little nose, her creamy skin and her silken hair, giving him one of her wry smiles and standing firm with her stubborn confidence. He could imagine the softness of her cheeks, feel the warmth of her skin … taste the sweetness of her lips.

"Arja."

He whispered her name, softly calling to her as he allowed his heart an instance of freedom.

The last thing he was expecting was her to answer him.

"What?"

Bjorn dropped his hammer as he whirled around, only to see the vibrant green eyes of Arja Freydottir alight with amusement as she looked at him.

14

<u>2</u>

◉ ◉ ◉

Arja clasped her hands behind her back, digging her fingernails into her palms, forcing back a laugh as she watched Bjorn compose himself. She had caught him off guard, and she enjoyed the sensation of doing so—especially since he'd surprised her, too.

When she'd made the decision to head over to his family's house, she had expected to wait for him to awake; it was still very early in the day, and even her youngest brother Frig was still asleep. But once Arja had seen the fire inside the forge, she felt a rush of vindication. The first spark of hope since Sterlig's death flared to life.

She had slipped into the forge, only to find Bjorn working diligently.

That was when her determination waned. Sweat glistened on his skin, and since he had rolled up his tunic sleeves, she could see the well-defined muscles of his forearms. Paired with the thoughtful determination on his face, he made it all too easy for her to stop and stare at him—just as his flustered reaction at finally seeing her made her smile.

"By the Allfather, Arja … I didn't know you—I mean, you're here, but … I could've hurt you." Bjorn hurried to pick up his hammer.

Arja smirked. "Are you certain of that? You seem fairly distracted."

"As opposed to unfairly, I presume?" Bjorn sighed, set down his hammer, and stepped forward, placing himself between Arja and the firepit.

He'd always been protective of her, Arja remembered wistfully while she watched him run his hands through his hair; she noticed it was growing longer, and the way it fell to his shoulders made her wish she could reach out and touch it.

The hope she'd felt earlier grew.

Is it possible Bjorn's forgotten about our last argument?

Arja curled her fingers into her fists. There was a line between hope and wishful thinking, she knew she was dangerously close to crossing it. Her hesitation increased when the thoughtful, contemplative look faded from Bjorn's face, and only a guarded expression remained.

"Why are you here?" Bjorn narrowed his eyes at her. "Did you need something repaired?"

"Yes, actually. But it's not something you can fix with your tools." Arja walked around the forge, taking note of the different tools. There were hammers and anvil stumps, various wedges, pliers, and tongs.

For all her determination, Arja knew she should've had a better plan. She could manage him when they were getting along; in some ways, he'd always been eager to please her. But now, it was harder to say if she could do so, especially considering their last encounter.

"It's too early for your riddles," Bjorn said. There was a new weariness in his voice, and Arja's temper flared.

"I'm sorry if I've interrupted your work, although I'm surprised you're out here this early."

"What it is you need, Arja?"

"I can leave if you want." Arja bit down on the inside of her cheek at her careless taunt, reminding herself she needed his help, and if she was going to get it, she had to be pleasant, especially because this was the first time they talked since the day before Sterlig had set sail for Eydis.

The memory scorched her mind again. She tried to push it away.

Bjorn turned back and spilled a small bucket of water onto the fire pit. Half the flames roared in protest; the other half died down.

"It might be early, but I couldn't sleep," Bjorn said. "I figured it was better to work."

He hadn't responded to her offer to leave, and she softened, grateful for his kindness again, no matter how begrudgingly he gave it.

"I would've done the same. And I know you like to work." Arja thought of reaching up and cupping his cheek, but she saw his eyes darken as she stepped closer to him again. He was still wary of her, and he had good cause. She gestured toward the anvil. "What have you been working on?"

He held up the small scythe he'd been hammering as she arrived.

"I lent it to Oleg last week," Bjorn explained. "I had my reservations, and it seems they were wise."

"I heard he had a small scuffle with Leif when they finished collecting the harvest for Kyvan's storehouses." Arja rolled her eyes. "Over Helga Arnesdottir, of all women."

"She's known for her beauty."

"But nothing else, Bjorn," Arja snapped. "She gets sick every year, mostly due to her own foolishness, and then expects everyone else to wait upon her every moment until she's better."

"Perhaps that is why Vidur didn't punish Oleg, even though a portion of grain reserves was lost during the battle." Bjorn finally smiled. "Helga will punish him when he marries her."

"It would be fitting." Arja glanced over at the small pile of broken tools on the nearby table. With the harvest season over, it wouldn't be long before Bjorn would be overwhelmed with requests to repair tools and commissions to sharpen or inscribe weapons. "And at least you have the scythe back."

"Not that it's needed as much, now that the harvest is over."

Before Arja could reply, the sword on the table caught her attention.

Sterlig's sword.

Arja shivered. Carefully, she reached for it, her fingers trembling as she took hold of it.

"I see you kept Sterlig's sword," Arja said. She tried to keep her voice light, but it still came out slightly strangled. Arja pulled the blade out of the scabbard, examining it carefully.

It was the same one her brothers described from their nightmares, the same sword she'd seen a hundred times in her own terrifying dreams. Every detail matched her memory, right down to the dried blood stuck inside the blade's decorative inscription.

"It's actually my sword," Bjorn told her. "Sterlig took it from me to go to Eydis."

"Well, that certainly sounds like him." Arja bit back a sigh as she ran her fingertips over the runic inscriptions on the blade. A slight whisper of ghostly green formed around the blade.

She looked up at Bjorn. Their eyes met, and a second later, she flinched.

"What is it?" Bjorn asked.

"Nothing." Arja pushed some of her loosened hair behind her shoulder and then sheathed the sword, trying to hide her lie. "I'll just never understand why you never took swordsmanship more seriously. You're strong enough to be a great warrior for Kyvan."

"There was never any need for me to fight," he said simply. "Not with Sterlig around."

"He never did like competing with you."

"No, he didn't." Bjorn finally reached out and took the sword back from her, letting his hands brush gently against hers.

Arja felt her heart skip a beat. "You should work on it more. You'd be good at it."

"Perhaps I will," Bjorn said with a small laugh. "Gilda mentioned that, too."

"Vidur's daughter?" Arja's brow furrowed. "The one who always walks around with her nose in the air, tossing her hair over her shoulder like a long horse tail?"

"Yes." Bjorn looked amused. "I spoke to her the last time I was in town. She'd asked me to take Sterlig's place in the chieftain's warriors."

"Oh, was that it?" Arja scoffed. "I'll bet she was really asking you into her bed."

"What?" Bjorn's mouth dropped open. "No, I'm sure it wasn't that."

"Oh, Bjorn." Arja giggled. "Gilda's not the only woman in town who's been paying you plenty of attention lately. Haven't you noticed at all?"

Bjorn shrugged, and Arja was incensed.

"They're all eager to know who you're going to marry, now that you're the only heir to your family's estate." Arja handed him the sword again before she crossed her arms. "Perhaps it might be easier for you to go viking, if you don't like the attention."

"You said it yourself, I didn't even notice it."

She had no way to know if he lied or not, but there was also no way to be sure unless she asked, and she would cut off her arm before asking Bjorn if he wanted more attention from the women in town.

"Besides, I don't have a need to pillage with the others," Bjorn added. "I'm happy to trade and smith for myself."

"You've never been one to take what belonged to others." Arja gave him a rueful smirk, and then she brightened. "I can teach you sword fighting if you want."

"Maybe."

"*Maybe*," Arja mimicked, rolling her eyes. "I'll have you know I'm one of the best shieldmaidens in Kyvan. Even Jarl Thordirsson says so, and you know how Vidur is with his compliments."

"It wasn't an insult," Bjorn assured her. He gave her a pat on the head, which only frustrated her more. "You know me very well, Arja. And you know I wouldn't dare insult you to your face."

"You could if you did it in such a subtle and nice manner that I missed it. I know how you are, with all the reading that you do."

"The runes and the sword both have their uses, and their own advantages. The sword has the power to take over a man's body, while stories can take over his mind." Bjorn laughed. "But today, in this case between us, I will declare you the winner, since you've managed to sidestep my questions impressively this morning."

"Do I get a prize for such a victory?" As if to tease him, Arja rounded on him, placing herself between him and the firepit. She'd meant to surprise him, but their closeness stunned her instead—and she was even more overwhelmed when her eyes met his, and his gaze lowered to her lips.

Her heart began to pound in her chest, and her breathing suddenly staggered.

"I'd give you a prize," Bjorn said slowly, "if I thought I could pay the price for it in the end."

Arja finally stepped around him again. "I'll take that to mean you owe me a favor."

Bjorn looked uneasy. "Why? What are you planning?"

"Nothing for you to worry about right now," Arja said. "I just like to keep track of my boons, Bjorn."

"When it's to your advantage," Bjorn pointed out. "You're quick enough to forget the ones you promise to others."

"That's not true!"

"It is, too," he insisted.

"Not *all* of the time."

"*Most* of the time." Bjorn leaned back and crossed his arms. "Why don't you tell me why you're even here in the first place, and *then* we'll decide who owes who favors?"

Arja's confidence dimmed. "Why wouldn't I be here? We're friends."

"If I recall our last conversation correctly, you never wanted to speak to me again."

Arja's cheeks flushed. "I was hoping we could forget that."

"It would be nice." The sadness in his voice reignited Arja's cautious hope until he added, "But Sterlig is dead now."

"That is exactly why we should move on." Arja clasped her hands together in front of her. "He's dead. And we are not. Not yet, anyway."

"Still—"

"Do you really miss him?" Arja asked, suddenly skeptical. "I know you didn't exactly get along."

Bjorn sighed. "I am sad that he is gone; my mother is in mourning, and my father is mad."

"I'll say he's mad." At the mention of Keyvak Ragnork, Arja couldn't stop a small chuckle. "Father has been saying for years if Keyvak wasn't such an amusing drunk and accomplished Viking, he would've been dead or disowned by our chieftain by now."

"My father is rude and rough, but there's no need to say he's insane. He is upset, not crazy."

"He *is* mad, Bjorn," Arja insisted.

Why does he have to take his father's side? Keyvak was hardly a supportive father to Bjorn, and the whole settlement of Kyvan knew it.

She sighed. "There's talk in the village about his temper, and I worry for you."

Bjorn looked back into the heart of the fire. "Is that why you're here? You wanted to come and check on me?"

"Not that you would appreciate it, but yes. Partially." Arja crossed her arms over her chest, drawing herself up to her full height. "I worry for plenty of people. And that is why I'm here. I need your help. It's about my brothers."

"Finn and Jon?"

Arja nodded.

"Will they be coming over, too?"

"What do you need with them?" Arja asked, annoyed. "What about my other seven brothers? Do you need Emil, Inor, Eir, Balder, Alfir, Gunnar, or Frig?"

"No." Bjorn rolled his eyes. "I was just asking."

"Perhaps you should've tried to sleep more."

"I'll never get enough sleep to deal with you, especially this early, Arja."

Arja stuck her tongue out at him before she thought better of it. Bjorn was likely just being kind, asking after her family, and she knew Jon and Finnar were among his closest friends.

But it was still grating, knowing she came second to her brothers.

Will he ever just pay attention to me?

When she saw him waiting for her to continue, she cleared her throat.

"I've been unable to sleep well since I learned of Sterlig's fate," Arja said slowly. "I dream of it sometimes."

There was a long moment of silence again, as Arja watched for his reaction. She had felt something strange in the air when she'd picked up Bjorn's sword, and once more, as she studied the redness of his eyes and the careworn lines drawn on his face, she felt something was amiss once more.

"I do, too."

Bjorn's voice was soft, and he turned away from her. "It's not because I'm weak."

"I wasn't going to say that."

"You weren't?" Bjorn arched his brow skeptically. "I find that difficult to believe."

"Well, I wasn't." Arja bit her lip, before she made her own confession. "I'm actually sympathetic to your plight. I've been having nightmares, too."

"I'm glad you told me." Bjorn's expression softened. "I don't feel quite so strange or alone."

"You've never been alone." On impulse, Arja reached out and embraced him. Bjorn went still, as the hard strength of her muscles and the soft welcome of her curves pressed against his body. She silently willed him to embrace her back, and finally, after what seemed like hours, his own smudged, callused hands tentatively tightened around her.

"I've always been here for you." She buried her head against his shoulder as he leaned into her hair.

"Have you?"

"Yes." Once again, regret over their last argument stabbed at her, and she cleared her throat. "And there's your mother. I know she's a good woman. And you had your Uncle Lodd, too."

"Thank you." He stepped back from her, and Arja's regret only grew.

She waited for him to say something, but after a long moment, she knew he would give her nothing else.

But there were other matters to see to, she reminded herself. Her brothers needed help, and now that Bjorn was no longer as upset with her, she had her opening.

"I'm glad you told me about the dreams," Arja said. "In fact, I'm certain now that it was exactly what I was waiting for."

"Waiting for?"

"Yes." Arja clenched her fists at her side. "I think we need to do something."

"About what?"

"Sterlig's death, of course."

Bjorn shook his head. "He's dead, Arja. There's nothing we can do about that."

"But think about it." Arja rounded on him. "We're having these awful dreams, aren't we?"

"My brother is still dead. There is no resurrecting him, Arja. Only one person has ever had the power to do that, and he will not help us now."

"But that doesn't mean we shouldn't do something. Even the Christian god has spoken through dreams before," she argued. "Think about it. Finn and Jon are both barely able to sleep, either, and we are all consumed with Sterlig's fate."

"What about your younger brothers?"

"Nothing's changed for them," Arja said. "*We* are the ones being called to act."

Bjorn studied her face, perhaps searching for any sign of deceit. She waited patiently.

But patience was not enough.

"You have to help me, Bjorn." She sighed as she admitted the real reason for her visit. "Jon tried to kill himself the other day."

"What?" Bjorn's eyes widened with concern. "What happened? Is he all right now?"

"He was down at the docks with the chieftain's other sailors. He fell into the water wearing a full set of armor." She bit her lip. "If the others hadn't seen him jump in, he would've died."

"I heard he'd had an accident, but I didn't think it was anything like that." Bjorn paced through the small forge.

"It wasn't an accident. My father has considerable influence, so that's the official story. But it's not the truth." Arja shook her head. "Mother was horrified. He's been bedridden for the last three days, having nightmares. He's called out for Sterlig to release him from Eydis' curse several times."

"I'm sorry," Bjorn said. "I didn't think to check on him."

"That's not your fault," Arja said. "But we do need to do something. Can't you see?"

Bjorn nodded. "All right. What do you have in mind?"

"Well … " Arja crossed her arms. "I think we should get married."

"What?" Bjorn stepped back, abruptly coming up against the edge of the firepit. "Ouch!"

Arja tried not to flinch. "My father wants me to get married, and marrying you is the easiest thing to do."

Bjorn coughed. "I don't think that's a good idea, Arja."

At his objection, the restraint on her temper snapped. "Oh, really? What do you think we should do about this, then?"

"Lacking courage is not the same as lacking sense," Bjorn argued back. "No man in his right mind will want to marry you, especially after what happened to my brother."

"Plenty of men want to marry me," Arja insisted, staring coldly at him. She flipped her hair over her shoulder.

"You're mad yourself," Bjorn argued.

Arja hurried toward the door. "I'm my mother's daughter, after all, and the very image of the goddess Freya herself."

"Every man wants to bed a goddess," Bjorn said. "No one wants to marry a spiteful shrew."

At that, Arja faltered as though he'd slapped her, and the pain of his words was hard, even if she knew she deserved it.

Bjorn looked just as surprised, and despite her anguish, Arja saw the remorse in his face.

"Never mind." Arja shook her head and pulled at her fur cloak. "I can see this was a waste of time."

"Arja, wait," he said. "I didn't mean—"

"No." Arja turned away from him, thrusting Sterlig's sword—*Bjorn's* sword—between them. "I don't need you to marry me. It was just one idea I had, that's all. And if you don't want to do anything about Sterlig, there's nothing I can do about that."

"It's not that—"

"I will take care of things myself." She stomped out of the forge. "You'll see."

"Arja, wait—" Bjorn followed after her. But before Bjorn could catch her, a slurred, drunken voice shouted his name from inside the main house.

"Bjorn!"

Arja finally stopped. She saw Bjorn's face had turned white, as they both realized his father was awake.

"I'm leaving," Arja said. Keyvak's temper rivaled her own, and it had only grown worse since Sterlig died. And as much as Bjorn infuriated her, she did not want him to get into any trouble.

"We aren't finished." Bjorn finally grabbed a hold of her shoulders, and his jaw clenched. "I'll come and talk with you later today."

"No." Arja pushed him away and slipped out of his grasp. "I have nothing else to say to you."

"Arja." Bjorn sighed. "Please, I don't want—"

A broad, shuddering shadow suddenly appeared in front of them, just as the dawn broke into the horizon. The first gleam of sunlight flickered off Keyvak's eyes; his gaze was full of rage as he looked at Arja.

"Well, if it isn't Frey's little shieldmaiden," Keyvak grumbled. "Come to collect what I owe your father, have you?"

<u>3</u>

❂   ❂   ❂

From where he was standing, Bjorn could see the redness in his father's eyes and the restlessness etched into the wrinkles of his face. Clearly, he was not in a good mood.

Of course, Keyvak Ragnork never bothered to be in a good mood for his second—and now only—son.

If Sterlig was alive, or even his Uncle Lodd, Bjorn would not have needed to deal with this kind of behavior from his father.

Bjorn shook his head. Sterlig complicated his life to no end, even in death.

"I came to see Bjorn," Arja replied. Her voice was firm and succinct, but Bjorn could tell she was struggling to hold back her anger.

"And she was just leaving." Bjorn quickly moved, stepping in front of her. He gave her a quick nod, indicating she should go—and hurry—if she wanted to get away without making the conflicts between their families worse.

Arja scowled up at him. "I can speak for myself."

"But you *were* just leaving, Arja," Bjorn reminded her. "Please don't make this worse."

"You're the one who's made it worse," Arja hissed as she shoved past both men, heading home.

Keyvak, for all the mead and ale he'd consumed, quickly grabbed her.

"You can go after I tell you what you've done to our family," Keyvak said. "How I lost Sterlig, and how I have to face the rest of my life without him, and how our crops aren't selling as much, how we've fallen into debt … "

Arja twisted away from him, and Bjorn hurried forward as Keyvak stumbled and fell.

His father landed hard on the cold ground and roared furiously.

Bjorn reached down to help him, but Keyvak only pushed him away.

"Leave me be," he snarled, before lunging after Arja again. "The wench should pay for the damage she's done."

Arja turned around, her eyes blazing. "How amusing, hearing such an argument from you, of all people, Keyvak Ragnork—the man known throughout all Kyvan for not paying his drinking debts."

Before Bjorn could stop him, Keyvak took hold of Arja; he caught her cloak and pulled hard.

Arja didn't hesitate. She pulled out a sword from under her cloak and positioned herself in a fighting stance.

Arja has my sword. Bjorn sighed. "Arja! That's mine—"

"You've got some nerve," Keyvak shouted, spewing another round of unfounded accusations at Arja as he grabbed at her again. "I won't have you coming after the rest of my family now that my son is dead."

"Stop, Father."

"I will not! Frey's daughter is nothing but a plague upon our family, and I will not rest until she is—"

Arja lunged forward, just as Bjorn finally caught up to his father. Bjorn swung his father back, throwing him back. Keyvak fell, and this time the impact knocked the wind out of him. Bjorn pinned him down as Arja's blow landed on his arm.

"Bjorn." Her lips parted in surprise while her eyes went wide.

Bjorn didn't have time to explain he'd only wanted to protect her before his father recovered enough to charge him.

"Arja." Bjorn twisted around between punches. "Go home. Please forgive him. He's drunk and doesn't know what he says."

"But I hurt you!" Arja raced forward, trying to pull Keyvak off Bjorn.

"It's not the worst wound you've give me." As his father grabbed him by the neck, Bjorn caught a glimpse of Arja's stricken expression and instantly regretted his words.

"It will be my last," Arja vowed before she sheathed the sword. She looked more defeated than ever as she met his gaze. "Goodbye forever, Bjorn."

He was about to remind her he would come to talk with her later, but his father threw him down again. Bjorn caught sight of the rock in his father's hand and ducked just in time.

The sharp edges of stone missed their impact, and at Keyvak's surprise, Bjorn cuffed his arms around his father's neck and squeeze hard.

Bjorn only loosened his grip when his father went limp. His father yielded, slumping over into the ground.

"I've won," Bjorn told him through gasping breaths. He reached forward to help him up, but Keyvak thrust his arm away.

"I don't need your help," he scoffed. "You might've won this battle, but I'm still drunk; if I were sober I'd kill you in a heartbeat."

"Mother will have to thank the Messiah for drunkenness then," Bjorn said, amused at the thought of his pious mother singing praises for such a sin.

His father's features only darkened. "You'll never be as good as Sterlig was. No matter how much you try to take his place in Arja's bed."

"I wouldn't do that to Sterlig." Bjorn did his best to ignore the stinging pain pouring from the wound Arja had dealt him.

"You've already proven your worthlessness," Keyvak grumbled.

Bjorn ignored his father's tirade. This was not the first time his father had declared Sterlig was dead because Bjorn had failed to go with him, or because Bjorn's sword was too weak, or because Bjorn himself was weak.

Keyvak would hound him for staying home and helping with the crops when he should've been out avenging Sterlig's death, and how in refusing to go, he'd dishonored the whole family and cursed Sterlig to remain outside Valhalla's eternal hall for eternity.

Even while his father yelled, Bjorn couldn't help but feel a little pity for him.

Keyvak had worked hard his entire life, all in hopes of passing his legacy down through a large family. When Sterlig was born, Keyvak had never felt so proud. But when Bjorn came, his mother barely survived giving birth. After two days of labor, Bjorn had been cut free of her. Since then, no other children had survived, let alone sons. Elska insisted they try for more, and she lost several other children through miscarriage and stillborn births.

After it became clear there were no more children to be had, Elska insisted Bjorn and Sterlig were enough, and that her other children would keep her company in the afterlife. She'd said before she loved Sterlig and Bjorn even more since it cost so much for her to have them, but Bjorn doubted Keyvak ever forgave him for being the last surviving son.

"I've come to a decision," Keyvak said, breaking into Bjorn's thoughts once more.

"What is it, Father?"

Bjorn studied his father. Beads of sweat formed on his forehead, and his cheeks were red and hollow, while the whites of his eyes were yellow. His brown hair, only a shade darker than Bjorn's, but now thinning with age, hung in limp strands. Keyvak coughed loudly, his entire body wracked with sickness.

Bjorn stepped up beside him, but Keyvak pushed him away.

"No," Keyvak snapped. "I don't want your help. Or you."

"Father—"

"Shut your mouth," he barked. "You feel sorry for me, but you don't do anything to help ease my pain. You sit around the house with your mother, feeling proud of your religion and your reading, believing you're everything *she's* ever wanted in a son, even if you're nothing to me. That's why you are no longer welcome here."

Bjorn remained quiet, but he felt nothing. No panic stirred inside of him, nor was there any urge to protest.

"Since you won't go and avenge Sterlig, you've proven to me that you're less than a son to me," Keyvak continued. "You're a farmhand, and nothing more. So leave. The harvest is over. Take your stuff and get out."

Bjorn was about to respond when his mother appeared outside. She had clearly been listening from the inside of the house; she still had a small kettle in her hand, as if she'd been in the middle of preparing tea.

"This is not acceptable, Keyvak!" she wailed. "You'd have my only son kill himself for you, when my other son is already dead."

"He wouldn't die for me," Keyvak scoffed. "No, he would die for honor. What good is our name, with Sterlig dead and Bjorn a coward?"

Bjorn flinched. It seemed Arja and his father, for all their animosity, shared the same opinion of him.

"What good is our name, if all our children are dead? Please, I need him here. There's too much to do without his help."

While Bjorn knew his mother was appealing to his father's benevolence in the way she knew best, it was still difficult to hear he was only welcome because he was useful.

"He can go be useful somewhere else, like a man," Keyvak snarled. "He's nineteen years old and still a child while he's clinging to you, Elska."

Arja thinks so, too. Perhaps it would be best to leave.

Bjorn stepped back as his mother continued to plead with his father.

"Please, Keyvak, you're not thinking this through," Elska pleaded.

"I have thought this through." Keyvak combed his fingers through his hair, trying to clean out the muddy strands he'd collected during their fight. "I've been thinking this through for many years. Where is this god of yours, who will give children to barren women such as yourself? With Sterlig gone and Bjorn still stuck at your side, there's nothing you can do but weep and pray, and that's given us nothing. Nothing!"

"Leave Mother out of this," Bjorn shouted angrily, as his mother's eyes filled with tears. "It's the only thing I ask, and I will leave in peace."

"There is no peace here for you to leave. And as for your mother, I'll do as I please with her, once you're gone, as is the right of her husband. Now, go!" Keyvak thrust his fists into Bjorn's chest.

Before Bjorn could retaliate, his mother slammed her cast iron kettle down on Keyvak's head. She stood there like a Valkyrie, wielding her heavenly weapon with divine grace and scourging displeasure as Keyvak fell to the ground, unconscious.

"You shouldn't have done that," Bjorn said, unable to shake off a sense of annoyance.

Arja and his own father had not believed that he could do the right thing. And now, his own mother had to protect him, too.

Elska shook her head. "Are you well, my son?"

"Yes."

"You're bleeding," she reminded him.

Bjorn watched as blood trickled down his arm and soaked through his woolen sleeve. There was a cut just above his elbow.

Arja's earlier attack.

Bjorn glanced over toward the fields, in the direction Arja had run. He rubbed a hand over his arm before placing it over his heart; his father wasn't the only one who needed to recover after the morning's debacle.

"Bjorn?" His mother touched his shoulder carefully. "What is it?"

Bjorn shook his head. He would bandage up his cut later. Ignoring his mother, he reached down and scooped up his father's fallen form.

"Where should I put him?" Bjorn asked.

Elska sighed. "I'd just as soon as leave him here to freeze."

"We are not like him." Bjorn grunted as he hauled his father over his shoulders and headed back into the house. "You and I were born to protect others, Mother."

Elska huffed. "It's not always a convenient trait. Put him in his bed, and I will see to him when he wakes."

"While you tend to him, I will pack my things," Bjorn said quietly.

"You don't have to do that, my son. I'm sure Keyvak will change his mind. Especially when he realizes that if you leave, he will have to do all the work around here."

"I said I would leave." He walked through the house toward his father's bed, and his mother followed him. "I will keep my word. I know you can take care of yourself, Mother, and there's no need to burden you unnecessarily."

"You are not a burden." Elska shook her head. "Even if it means we have to handle Keyvak's anger."

"With me gone, perhaps he will be less angry, and he'll be able to work more," Bjorn said. "And if he does work, he might even stop drinking."

"The sun will die out first."

Bjorn smiled. "Still, I am old enough to start my own family, Mother. Perhaps in his own way, Father is trying to do what is best. Even Uncle Lodd said I would be on my own soon, before he died. And … I think it's time I did something about

Sterlig's death, too. God has given you peace, but I believe he is calling me to find it on my own."

Bjorn thought of the nights when he'd spent dreaming of his brother's death. He had woken up resolved, but then his daytime concerns had overruled his roughened certainty.

Arja had been right, he conceded silently. He would have to do something—and the first thing he had to do was figure out just what that meant.

Elska said nothing, but her tears finally fell free from her tired eyes and she nodded.

As he placed his father on his pallet, Keyvak stirred slightly, and Bjorn knew he would have to hurry; it wouldn't be long before his father would awaken.

After he bandaged his arm, Bjorn packed a large bag, with what clothes he could, leaving behind what he knew he could gain through trade. He balanced the bag on his round shield and tied them to his back.

When he'd finished inside, Bjorn walked out to the forge and bundled up several of his tools. His skills in metalworking and smithing would be the easiest ways to earn a living.

It was as he finished packing his hammer that he remembered Arja.

She still has my sword.

Bjorn sighed; he would have to get it back when he went to see her.

He would do that, and then after he made it clear to Arja he would never be a substitute for Sterlig, he would go into town.

Bjorn straightened his shoulders. It was always better to have a plan. It gave him hope to have one, even if he had no way of knowing just how it would work out.

Just as he was about to leave, the door to his home slammed open with a defiant, deafening sound.

"Bjorn!"

His father was awake.

"Time to leave," Bjorn murmured as he made his way out of the forge for the last time and headed out from the only home he'd ever known.

He wasn't far when his mother came running up behind him. She embraced him, not without some difficulty due to his pack, but she held onto him tightly.

Bjorn hugged her back. It was cold, but while he was not wearing a cloak, he felt the warmth he'd always associated with her as they held each other. He let that essence of her sink into his memory, willing himself to carry it with him throughout the rest of his days.

A low growl called out from the house, and he looked up to see Keyvak appear in the doorway.

"God bless you, my son." Elska let her arms fall away from his shoulders.

"I love you," Bjorn replied. "Goodbye, Mother."

"Take this," Elska whispered, stuffing her hand into his pack while she held onto him once again. Bjorn realized she was trying to hand him something so his father wouldn't see. "Trade it for passage on a ship."

"No," Bjorn said. "If you have something to trade, it should be put toward what Father owes the Gilssons."

Elska ignored him. "If you leave Kyvan, you could try to go to Oseberg. You might be able to find my father's family there."

"I don't want to sail to another country," Bjorn said. "I'd rather stay in Kyvan."

"Oh, Bjorn. I suppose I knew you would want to stay close by. After all, you love her, don't you?"

Bjorn froze, stunned by his mother's unexpected comment. "Her?" he repeated, his voice sounding unintelligible to his own ears.

Elska gave him a kind smile, and there was a new brightness in her eyes. "Arja, of course. I've known since the day you met her that she was special to you, Bjorn. She might have only seen Sterlig for a while, but if you want to wed her, you have my blessing—"

"But not Sterlig's."

"He is dead, Bjorn." Elska ducked her head. "I know you worry about his honor, but he always took care of it on his own. Leave it behind."

THE LEGEND OF EYDIS

Bjorn busied himself by putting on his cloak. "It doesn't matter now. I doubt Arja feels the same."

"Only a woman can truly tell you what is in her own heart," Elska said. "Don't be too sure of what you think when it comes to her."

Bjorn thought of Arja's earlier visit. He had a feeling his mother would be shocked to learn just what Arja did think. She'd suggested they wed in hopes of appeasing Sterlig's spirit, to cure her brothers of their nightmares over Sterlig's death. He would be a replacement husband and lover, without any true love between them. The way she talked, it was no more than switching out a broken axle for a working one, and Bjorn would never agree to such a fate, no matter how much he loved her.

"Thank you." He gave his mother one last kiss on the cheek.

Elska's eyes filled with tears again, but he would only hurt her more if he allowed their farewells to go on any longer. Back in the house, he heard his father growl.

"Take care of yourself," Bjorn said, taking her hand and squeezing it one last time.

Leaving his mother hurt more than anything else, but she had done everything she could to give him peace. He did not look back, pressing forward one step at a time.

As he walked, he pulled out the small bag she had stuffed into his pack. He had expected some coins or some choice cuts of meat; instead he was surprised to find her golden crucifix.

"Mother."

He tightened his grip on the small cross. The golden chain dangled from his grip as he stared at it. He was almost tempted to go and give it back to her, but he knew such a gesture would only hurt his mother more. Instead, he carefully wrapped the chain around the center of the cross and then placed it back in its bag. Once it was securely tied to his belt, next to where he usually kept his sword, Bjorn vowed he would honor her wishes, as he always had.

After he dealt with Arja.

48

4

The nerve of him.

Arja pushed another tunic into her pack, desperate to keep from breaking out into sobs as she packed. In spite of her best efforts, a few, slim tears leaked out of her eyes, blurring her vision and forcing her to falter in her task.

A small whimper cried out from behind her, and for a moment, Arja went rigid and stiff, desperately hoping she hadn't woken up one of her many younger brothers. When a paw clawed at her leg, she fell to her knees, already embracing the loyal pup at her heels.

"Oh, Ulf," she murmured, burying her face into his soft and slightly dirty fur. He licked the tears off her face, and normally, she would have smiled.

But today, it was not enough.

"I know you're hungry," she said, pulling away. "I'd feed you before I leave, but I already know Gunnar and Balder will stuff you until you're nice and plump once I'm not around to watch them."

Her two younger brothers, not even eight summers old, were always sneaking Ulf a spare scrap of food, no matter how many times Arja and her mother chastised them. They played roughly at times, but Arja knew they loved the dog as much as she did.

She gave Ulf another pet. "It's a good thing I have a job for you while I'm gone."

Ulf whimpered again, but this time Arja went back to packing up her bag.

"Don't be too sad. I'll need you to be extra careful while I'm gone. You'll be watching over Jon." She glanced over at the far wall of her room, where her brother continued to rest and recover from his near-death.

Ulf curled at her feet, and Arja went back to work.

It was too easy to pick out her clothes from the mess of laundry; as the only daughter, she was constantly given dresses and aprons to wear, though she also had her own set of breeches and boots. As she looked through the different piles of clothes pulled in from their washing, Arja also grabbed Finnar's hunting shirt. Her brother's tunic was thicker than hers, and the extra protection and padding could also help with her fight against the dragon.

"Finn won't mind," she muttered to herself.

Finnar was her older brother and closest to her in age. She had been following after him all her life, and he never seemed at odds with having a second shadow.

THE LEGEND OF EYDIS

It was thanks to Finnar, and her other older brother, Jon, that she'd meet Bjorn and Sterlig in the first place. They'd been paired together one summer, when the chieftain had called for their generation of warriors to begin training.

Arja scowled. She hated thinking of Bjorn. His painful rejection pushed against her all once more.

She'd gone to see him, believing if she talked with Bjorn, it would give her some peace at last, only to be called a shrew and to engage in a skirmish with her family's largest debtor.

And now she was alone in her quest. Bjorn was not going to help her.

Instead he'd humiliated her.

Anger resurged, its heat full of ice, as Arja grabbed her round shield.

Bjorn should've agreed to help me.

A small part of her knew he was dedicated to seeing to his family's care first and foremost; after all, he was an honorable man with a good reputation, even if others thought he was weak compared to Sterlig. She'd seen him in Kyvan, trading his services and metalworking for low pay—all so his beast of a father could drink himself further into madness each night, apparently, and all while women like Gilda used Bjorn for their amusement.

She paused in her movements, stuffing her coin purse into her cloak, thinking of how Bjorn had looked at her when she'd embraced him and reliving that moment of heat as she stood there, waiting for him to kiss her.

Arja had watched him carefully; she knew he wanted to—but then he stopped himself, for some reason, and stepped out of her reach.

Yes, Bjorn was an honorable man.

Perhaps too honorable.

Arja sighed and headed out of her room, careful not to make any noise as she walked toward the longhouse's pantry. She did not want anyone else to know of her early trek into the Kyvansson land, and she certainly did not want them to interrupt her as she prepared to leave.

She froze as she heard a small sniffle.

Arja held her breath as she waited, wondering if it was already too late.

After another few sniffles and a sneeze, Arja shook her head. Frig, her mother's latest babe, had been born at the start of the harvest, just a week before Sterlig left for Eydis, and he was on the verge of waking up.

I'll have to hurry.

As the only daughter in a household of ten children, Arja was tasked with taking care of her younger siblings, and she rightfully resented the job. As Finnar and Jon learned to fight, sail, and hunt, she would sneak off with them whenever she could. Finnar helped her escape more than once, and later on, even Sterlig and Bjorn provided other opportunities for her to leave.

As Arja gathered up some dried fish and berries, she thought about those early days, about learning how to use a sword and shield. Her brothers had been loud and argumentative, and Sterlig had always been the champion among their group. Bjorn had never wanted to fight her. She nearly always won when she finally goaded him into a duel, and when she didn't, he always looked more upset when they finished. After Bjorn went to train with his uncle, he always found a way to avoid fights.

Remembering how he had practically run from the thought of marriage to her, Arja gritted her teeth. She clung to the hatred she felt for him, knowing it was the only thing keeping back the deep shame in her heart.

A baby's cry cut through her concentration.

"Oh, no." Arja scrambled back to her room as she heard Frig's waking cries. It would only be a matter of seconds before—

"Arja! Can you get the baby?"

Geira, her mother, was awake as well.

"I'll be there in a moment." Arja put down her supplies and swept Ulf into her arms before slipping into Jon's room.

As the eldest brother, Jon had always been the one who carried the most promise as Frey Gilsson's heir.

She crept into his room and stood over him, feeling more like a mother than a sister as she mopped up his brow and allowed Ulf to jump on his bed.

Jon stirred. "It's the princess, Sterlig. She's bewitched you, and now she's come for me … "

Arja giggled softly. "I'm no witch."

Jon blinked, and in the soft morning light, his blue eyes seemed to burn a tired violet as he looked up at her. "Arja? Is that you?"

"Of course it's me." She sat down next to him. "You're still sleepy, are you?"

Jon shook his head. "I'd rather be dead," he whispered.

"It's only a matter of time, but Mother and the rest of us would prefer a longer time," Arja said, trying to keep her voice light.

She knew of the nightmares, but she had never set foot on Eydis. She imagined Jon's dreams carried much more certainty than hers.

"I've brought Ulf with me, so he can watch over you while I'm gone," Arja said.

"Are you going into town again?" Jon pulled his blanket over his head. "You've been going there a lot."

"You know how it is. Camille's always good for a story, and he's only here a couple days every week." Arja thought of her friend from Eydis and smiled.

"Father's not out of Mother's perfume already, is he?" Jon asked.

"You know our parents. Mother loves him enough to drown herself in his gifts, and he's fool enough to give her the opportunity to do so."

Arja regretted her joke, but when Jon laughed harder, she let it slide.

Frig cried out from the other room, and Arja sighed. She stood up and pressed a kiss to her brother's forehead. "I've got to go. Take care of yourself while I'm gone."

Jon nodded and yawned. In the dim morning light, Arja could see the smile he gave her, and the weakness of it made her want to hit him. He was her older brother, and the former pride of their family. He was training with the chieftain to be one of Snæland's finest warriors, and he was already an excellent sailor on their viking trips. And unlike Sterlig, he was humble about his triumphs, so his stories were always more believable.

Despite the rage she felt at the injustice he faced, Arja had to leave it behind her as she picked up her very wiggly, very unhappy baby brother.

"Shh, Frig," she murmured, picking him up out of his bed and holding him close.

When he stopped squirming, Arja felt a rush of pride. No one could take care of her brothers the way she did.

She bounced the baby in her arms and rocked him as she studied her home. Her family history was fraught with stories of fighting the elements to ensure survival. Her blood was mixed with those who went into battles, and the sweat of those who worked the fields. The mothers and daughters passed on the families' stories from generation to generation.

This was the place where she had been born, the place where she grew up—the place where she would always be welcomed by her blood.

And now she was leaving it.

"Arja?"

At the sound of her mother's call, Arja could not stop herself from wishing she had already left. She had attended to her fate dutifully as always, even if she wearied at the thought.

"I'm here," Arja said. "I've got Frig."

"Thank you," Geira said, appearing slightly disheveled, still in her sleeping gown. "I will need you to tend to the meal while I feed him."

Arja bit her lip. "No. I have to go today, Mother."

"Where? To town?"

"Yes."

"You're certainly energetic this morning." Geira smiled wanly, pushing Arja's loose hair behind her ear as she came up next to her. "Couldn't sleep? Were you dreaming of your Sterlig again?"

"No." Arja nearly choked. She hoped her clipped tone would encourage her mother to refrain from saying anything else; from the smell emitting from her brother, she had enough unpleasantness before her.

Geira glanced back up at Arja and said, "You didn't wake up because of Finn or Jon, or their nightmares, did you?"

"No." She bit her lip. It was not a lie, since her own nightmares had roused her. "How is he? What about Jon?"

"Jon has been resting more peacefully today," Geira admitted. "I imagine he will not be able to work for another week yet."

"Maybe he's just using this as an excuse," Arja suggested, only half in jest, making her mother gasp.

"Oh, Arja." Geira sighed, and the light in her eyes dimmed as she glanced over at the shared room where Finnar and Jon slept. "How I wish they had never gone to Eydis."

Guilt and shame burrowed into Arja. She wondered all over again if she should've tried to stop Finnar and Jon from sailing with Sterlig. She heard them leave that night, but before she could follow, Frig, born only the week before, had started to cry.

Geira had called Arja for help, and she'd been stuck between choosing to go after her older brothers or help her mother tend to her newest one.

Arja wondered, along with a thousand other things, if she'd made the right choice that night.

"Mother, will our family ever return to normal?" Arja asked.

"There is no normal any longer, I am afraid," Geira said quietly. "There is no normal after losing a child."

"You haven't lost—"

"Haven't I?" Geira shrugged. "Jon is alive, as is Finnar. That's true, thank Odin. But some part of them has been lost, and they are not the same. And neither are you, are you?"

At the look in her mother's eye, Arja knew she was trapped.

Giving in, Arja sighed. "I still can't talk to Elska."

Arja, like the rest of Kyvan and the surrounding settlements, knew Bjorn's mother had gone through several miscarriages and stillborn births. Arja couldn't imagine her pain in losing her oldest son to the dragon of Eydis.

An image of Bjorn's sword—the one Sterlig had carried to Eydis—flashed through Arja's mind. She could see the blood on the blade as it sank into the runic inscriptions; she could see a ghoulish tint to the sword as Finnar carried it down to Eydis' only port, where the knarr and her family's last thralls were eagerly waiting to leave.

She had dreamed it hundreds of times now.

Geira put her hand on her cheek, startling her. "Women were made to give life, and we were born to carry its burdens. Our hearts might be broken, but we still carry the broken hearts of others. It is the way of things, *dúllan mín*."

Arja handed Frig over to her mother, just as Frig began to smell. "Is there any good reason to be a woman at all then?"

Geira smiled, this time much more brightly. "When you have found a good man, one to whom you can trust your heart, mind, and body, you will see things differently. Love like your father and I share can transform any pains into the deepest joys. Isn't that right, my darling Frig?"

Arja watched as her mother's eyes lit up, even as Frig's face contorted, and he defecated again.

If her mother's love for her father could make baby excretion something to smile over, Arja had to admit her mother was right.

Either that, or she's mad.

But then, Arja recalled ruefully, her mother wasn't the one having nightmares about an island she'd never seen and a dragon that wasn't supposed to be real.

"Perhaps it would help your brothers if you were to wed, Arja. They might fear you are upset with them for Sterlig's death."

A large, unpleasant lump rose in Arja's throat. Now that Bjorn rejected the idea of marrying her, it was time to leave that possibility behind.

"I had my own ideas of what to do to help them," Arja said. "I've been thinking over some ideas."

Behind them, a new voice let out a small snort. "Well, that's never good, is it?"

Geira and Arja turned to see Finnar standing behind them. His blue irises were surrounded by red, as dark circles dragged down his eyes, and his black hair was as wild as their mother's.

"We all know there's only trouble coming, if Arja's thinking," Finnar said.

"At least I'm able to think." Arja crossed her arms over her chest.

"Perhaps it's better if I don't think so much. My life will be simple then," Finnar said.

"I'm not sure how it can get any simpler."

"Enough," Geira interjected. She stepped between her children and scowled. "The way you two fight makes me wonder if you'll ever be ready for families of your own."

"Why mess with perfection?" Finnar asked, pressing a kiss to her cheek, even if the smile on his face failed to light up his eyes. He nudged Arja in a brotherly manner. "And we all know Arja's never going to marry anyone. Talk about being simple— no one could be that dense."

Normally, Arja would have laughed and agreed with him, but this time she said nothing, and her hands began to tremble.

Geira tightened her lips. "That's enough. There are plenty who would be proud to marry Arja."

"Mother, please." Arja shook her head. "Not this. Not now."

"Oh, my sweet girl." Geira's eyes filled with tears. "I know how sad you still are. We don't mean to trivialize your pain over Sterlig's loss."

Finnar's face blanched at hearing Sterlig's name. He turned away and faced the burning firepit in the center of the house.

And at that, Arja squared her shoulders. "I've made a decision. I'm going to go to Eydis."

Geira gasped, while Finnar spun to stare at her, but Arja tightened her jaw. Only Frig, oblivious to the gravity of the situation, continued to wriggle and whine in his mother's arms.

"What?" Finnar's mouth dropped open. "No, Arja. It's too horrible."

"It can't be that horrible," Arja scoffed. "Camille and Ephraim live there, and they've sailed there many times. I'm going to go back with them to Eydis when they cast off later today."

"Your friends are *from* Eydis," Finnar said. "If they didn't come here to trade their perfume, we'd kill them the moment their boat pulled into port."

"They can help me," Arja said. "And with their help, I'll slay the dragon."

"By the gods, you are daft." Finnar jutted his finger into her chest. "Sterlig was a much better warrior than you, and *he died*. Countless others have, too."

"I know that!" Arja snapped. "I know all about the legend."

"Oh, Arja, my sweet child, you've always been too eager to go chasing after daydreams." Geira sighed heavily.

"Day schemes, more like it," Arja said. "But in this case, people are suffering, and I need to do something about it—and this is the only way now."

"Now?" Finnar asked, arching his brow skeptically.

Arja would rather cut out her own tongue and cook it for dinner than tell Finnar what had happened with Bjorn earlier.

"It's been long enough. I'm over my grief for Sterlig," she said instead, making Finnar turn away from her. Arja knew he wasn't able to face her pain at Sterlig's loss, any more than she could take his nighttime terror. "All the men who've gone to Eydis before have failed. Perhaps a shieldmaiden will succeed."

"But the dragon—"

"There are worse things in life than dragons, Finn," Arja snapped. "Including watching you and Jon skirt around Kyvan like skittish horses and having Jon try to drown himself. And as much as I—you might hate it, you're right: no one here wants to marry me. Not now that Sterlig's dead."

Arja hated how her voice nearly cracked as she hinted at her pain of Bjorn's rejection. She would not tell them the details, but she was going to make it clear she had to go. She brushed a lock of hair out of her face, grabbing at a moment to compose herself.

"What else can I do?" she asked. "I will gladly sacrifice myself for those I love. And that even includes you and Jon, Finn. Shockingly."

After a resounding silence, Finnar sighed bitterly in defeat. "Well, the gods know you don't fight fair. Perhaps you will win."

"Thank you." Arja smirked, taking his insult as a compliment.

She turned to face a heartbroken Geira. "I'm sorry, but I have to do this. You can ask Elska to help! I'm sure Bjorn's mother would be willing to take my place here. And there are other thralls to help with the boys, too. Please don't try to stop me."

"Oh, Arja." Geira shook her head. "I have never been able to stop you before, my sweet

THE LEGEND OF EYDIS

shieldmaiden. But can you look me in the eye and vow before the gods that this is what you truly want?"

Arja thought back to Bjorn and then nodded fiercely. If she had to go battle with her brothers' ghosts, or if she had to face off the dragon of Eydis herself, she would.

Anything for my family. She tightened her fingers into fists. *Anything to stop feeling all this guilt.*

"Yes," Arja said. "Yes, this is what I want."

"You're mad!" Finnar exclaimed. "Mother, are you really going to let her go like that?"

"It is her choice." Geira shook her head slowly. "If you want to stop her, you'll have to do it yourself, Finn. Your father's away on another viking trip, and I have eight other sons to care for, and Arja is old enough to decide her own destiny now."

"Don't even try."

"It's possible she might yet change her mind, too." Geira glanced at Arja, who only winced at her mother's pleading expression.

She'd had a feeling her mother was hoping she would change her mind on her own. But Geira would be disappointed, even though Arja hated to do that to her.

"I've made my decision." Arja turned her focus back to Finnar and glared at him. "You won't win."

"I will stop you," Finnar insisted. "I'll get Bjorn to help me."

Arja scowled. "Why would you bother wasting your time with him at all? I can win against a weakling like him anytime."

"No wonder you think you'll be able to defeat the dragon guarding Eydis," Finnar said. "Are you really that blind and foolish, Arja? Bjorn *lets* you win when you battle him. He doesn't like hurting you."

Arja put her hands on her hips, defiant. "He wins some of the time."

"Enough you don't realize he's tricking you," Finnar muttered.

"You're lying." Arja shook her head, determined not to hear anything else. She had made a gamble when it came to asking Bjorn to marry her, and she'd lost. She would not lose anything else to him—not when he'd already made it clear he wouldn't fight for her before. "And even if what you're saying is true, Bjorn won't stop me from going to Eydis. He's got his life here to get on with."

Finnar rolled his eyes. "I don't think you know Bjorn as well as you think you do."

"Well, I don't think you or Bjorn know me as well as you think you do, either," Arja snapped, turning away and heading toward her room. "Which isn't that much of a surprise, given Sterlig's delusions."

"What are you talking about?" Finnar asked.

Arja clamped her mouth shut, horrified she'd said anything. She pushed past him, nearly knocking him over as she grabbed her pack and her shield—and Bjorn's sword—before she finally left her home.

Finnar called after her, but she ignored him, desperate to escape before she broke down in tears and confessed the dark secrets she had, the ones that were slowly devouring her own heart.

THE LEGEND OF EYDIS

<u>5</u>

◎　　◎　　◎

Bjorn walked slowly through the woods between his family's home and the Gilsson lands. He kept his steps light against the hardening chill of the ground, listening intently for any sound behind him.

Knowing his father watched from their turf house, Bjorn had quickly made his way to the cover of the woods. But once he was out of Keyvak's sight, Bjorn turned and watched the house for some time, wanting to make sure his mother would be all right. He could hear her weeping inside before his parents began to argue over chores and coins and other things.

He had no idea how much time had passed before Keyvak finally left the house and began chopping wood for their fire pit, but upon seeing his father work, Bjorn decided to move on.

He prayed his father would be good to his mother and that Keyvak would fulfill his duty to Elska in at least an honorable way, if not a loving one.

Bjorn moved onward slowly, still keeping an ear out for any trouble behind him, knowing full well there would be only trouble ahead of him when he talked with Arja again. The cut on his arm she'd accidently given him tingled under his bandage, as if in silent agreement.

Bjorn stepped out of the shadow of the woods and arrived at the Gilsson land. He almost smiled at the thought of seeing their longhouse, remembering the fun he'd had as a child, playing with Finnar and Jon and Arja, and even Sterlig, too.

And then Bjorn recalled how Sterlig had bragged, only weeks before his death, how much Keyvak liked the idea of expanding their turf house into a longhouse like the one owned by the Gilsson family. Sterlig said that alone would smooth over Keyvak's distaste for his choice of bride.

Bjorn stopped walking, irritated by the thought of Arja married to Sterlig, and further despaired at the thought that he would have been forced to help construct the new lodge.

"Bjorn!"

Bjorn looked up at the familiar voice, only to see Finnar as he appeared at the edge of the woods, running toward him at a rapid pace. Even with the trees and distance between them, Bjorn could see Finnar was wearing a large pack on his back along with a round shield.

"Finn!" Bjorn called back to his friend, grateful to see him.

In the past several months, following Sterlig's death, Finnar had remained distant and constantly nervous, never wanting to go far from his house, and vehemently avoiding the port at Kyvan. Bjorn had tried to visit with him a few times during the busy harvest season, but Finnar always found a way to excuse himself after a short time.

Watching as Finnar stumbled toward him, Bjorn wondered if his friend was starting to return to his regular self.

"Whoa!" Finnar slipped in the muddy ground, and nearly fell over as he stopped before Bjorn.

Bjorn quickly steadied him. "It's good to see you, Finn. How are you faring?"

Bjorn regretted his question as he saw the frantic terror in his friend's eyes; something serious was bothering his friend.

"Oh, Bjorn, thank the gods you're here," Finnar said. "Come with me and hurry."

"What is it?" His heart beat wildly at the thought of Arja. "Is it … Jon? He is well?"

"No, he's fine. Well, mostly. He's alive anyway." Finnar coughed, before he cleared his throat. "I suppose Arja told you what happened to him?"

"Yes. She was very upset about him earlier."

"You saw her today?"

"Well … " A sense of unease stirred inside his gut.

Finn isn't here to defend Arja's honor, is he?

"Never mind." Finnar shook his head. "That doesn't matter now. Arja's gone."

"Gone?"

"Yes." Finnar crossed his arms over his chest. "She's been mad with guilt, and she's decided to go to Eydis."

No. Bjorn reached for his sword, only to remember Arja had taken it from him earlier.

"You should've seen her, Bjorn. She just announced to me and Mother that she was going to go to Eydis. She could have just as easily been talking about visiting port, or even going on a raid. I tried to talk some sense back into her, but she wouldn't listen."

"That sounds like Arja." Bjorn grimaced and looked toward Kyvan, where the nearest port of Snæland was just beyond another set of hills. "If she's headed for Eydis, we'd better get to port."

The tilled farmland of the Gilsson land blended into the rocky trails, and soon the port city of Kyvan came into full view from the hills outside the city. As they paused at the top of another mount, Bjorn could smell the cold scent of the northern seas, its salty bitterness a sign of death as well as life.

Finnar nudged him as they headed into the city. "This is all your fault, you know."

"What?" Bjorn scowled at him. "My fault?"

"Yes." He pushed some of his long black hair out of his face. "You should've just married her."

"I can't just marry her so she can forget about Sterlig—"

"No, that's not what I meant," Finnar said. "You should've just married her, before all this happened."

"Finn … " Bjorn did not want to discuss this with Arja's brother, let alone anyone else. His earlier conversation with Arja still mystified and annoyed him.

"My sister is honorable enough, isn't she?"

"Of course she is," Bjorn hurriedly assured him. "But—"

"You should've just asked before all of this started. Sterlig and me and Jon wouldn't have gone to Eydis in the first place, and Arja wouldn't feel so compelled to go and avenge Sterlig's death."

Bjorn felt his heart race again, this time with terror. "What makes you think I like her?"

"Stop that. We know you do—"

"We?"

"Jon and I, who do you think?" Finnar groaned as they walked down the hill, resuming their trek. "That was part of the reason we didn't think Sterlig was serious about Arja—not until he decided to go to Eydis, anyway. We figured you'd object eventually, even if Sterlig managed to kill the dragon. By the gods, I thought you'd even try to take her while Sterlig was gone."

"I … " Bjorn felt his ears burn. He was unable to stop himself from recalling the argument he'd had with Arja while Sterlig was away on Eydis, the last time he'd seen her before earlier that morning.

Arja had come to see him, bragging to him how Sterlig was going to slay the dragon of Eydis for her, and how she loved Sterlig so much, and how there was nothing Bjorn could do to stop them from wedding.

When he offered her a reluctant, defeated congratulations—the only thing he knew that would irritate her as much as she was annoying him—she only grew more obnoxious and dared him to take her then and there. When he refused to play her game and dishonor his brother, their conversation quickly devolved into a shouting match, one Arja supposedly won when she cursed at him and told him she never wanted to speak with him again.

"What is it?" Finnar asked.

"Forget it." Bjorn shrugged. "Let's just get to the port. If she's going to Eydis, she'll need a ship. And that means she'll talk with the perfume traders."

Bjorn was grateful their conversation steered away from Arja as they made their way toward the port. The island of Snæland was far away from the rest of the known world, removed enough that the only real troubles that came from other lands were whispers and rumors. Many of the ships at port were locally owned and built, and the life of Kyvan rested in the arms of the sea and her generosity.

THE LEGEND OF EYDIS

But a few foreign trade ships would appear in port at regular intervals ranging from days to months. One such ship was the *Sea Serpent*, owned by the perfume traders from Eydis. Every twelve days, without fail, it came to port with its cargo hold bursting with soaps, perfumes, and other goods made from the strange flowers that only grew on the island.

The bright crimson sail of the famous ship hung down from its mast, and even from a distance, Bjorn could see the small crew finishing their noontime chores. They came each week, stayed for no longer than three days, and then headed back to their home to collect another shipment.

Bjorn looked around, a sense of fear adding to his ache to find Arja.

The pack on his back briefly jostled, diverting his attention for a moment when he saw some smithing tents. He had planned to make a living in the city, now that he was on his own, and the sight of their storefront made him pause.

"Where is she?" Finnar's voice nearly cracked as he came up beside Bjorn, his eyes round and redder than ever before, with large beads of sweat forming on his brow.

"Are you well, Finn?" Bjorn asked.

"Arja's going to get herself killed if she goes to Eydis and tries to avenge Sterlig." Finnar elbowed him. "You can't let her die."

"What makes you think she'll listen to me?" Bjorn clenched his jaw, thinking of their earlier encounter again.

"Because you're Sterlig's brother."

"You're *her* brother."

"She won't listen to me. Or our mother. We already tried." Finnar narrowed his gaze at Bjorn. "I'm sure she has been probably pretty awful to you these last few months, and I offer you my full apologies and my sympathies, Bjorn. Having grown up with her at my heels I know what a beast she can be. But you can't be so upset with her that you'd let her get into trouble."

Knowing her as he did, Bjorn figured it had only been a matter of time before Arja found trouble, but Finnar was right. He might've been upset with Arja and her earlier flippancy, but he would do anything to protect her—no matter the cost.

"All right," Bjorn said. "Let's head over to the *Sea Serpent*. That's the boat that goes to Eydis, and they should be leaving port today."

"If they're leaving today, we'd better hurry," Finnar said. He eyed the clouds and gulped. "It looks like a storm is coming in."

Arja eyed the side of the *Sea Serpent* skeptically and then turned to the dark-skinned man beside her. "I'm not sure. I think I can do better."

"You think you can do better? Ha! I think not."

While Camille had traded with her often enough in the past for her to know he was actually giving her a fair deal, her trader's instincts ran deep, and she wanted her last deal on Snæland to be a good one.

"I must remind you, my friend, that this is the only trade ship that goes to Eydis." Camille laughed, his large belly shaking as he looked down at her. He was an older man, but despite his age, he carried an air of youthfulness about him. "Unless, of course, you've done the smart thing and changed your mind?"

"The smart thing in this instance is not the right thing." Arja smiled bitterly at her friend. "So I'd appreciate a better price if you can give it."

Camille sighed. "Stubborn as always, I see."

"As the storm," Arja agreed, glancing up to the sky.

"The storm is less intimidating."

Arja grinned up at him, and despite the tension over their haggling, they shared a laugh.

Camille was the kind of man who enjoyed talking with anyone, and Arja was grateful for his cheerfulness. She'd met him the previous year, when, after Geira announced she was pregnant with

Frig, her father set out to buy some perfume from the Eydis traders. Since then, Arja had been allowed to come to the port with her father. Frey Gilsson, being a man of means with a lot of offspring, had a good reputation, and the merchants and traders were always willing to speak with Arja, even if she had nothing to trade.

Things had changed since Sterlig's death, and even her father's riches as a trader weren't enough to help her buy any goodwill. Many of the people nearby turned away as she approached, or else they failed to meet her eye when they talked—unless they were content to voice their disapproval of her aloud. Gilda, the oldest daughter of the chieftain and one of Sterlig's former devotees, was among the first to exclude Arja from any social gatherings after Sterlig's funeral.

Arja hated to think what they would do if the townsfolk found out about Jon's attempt on his life. She was thankful for her family's company, and her friends like Camille; she was certain that she would've gone truly mad if the older sailor hadn't welcomed her discussions whenever he came to port.

Arja looked over at Camille's ship, with its renowned longship build and its red-purple sail, its distinctive dragon design tailored into its fabric. The remnants of Eydis' famous scent flowed out from the ship, offering her an empty but comforting reminder that, despite the painful story of Princess Brynja and the tragic loss of Prince Andor, Eydis was still home to many beautiful mysteries. There were whispers that the perfume was the essence of true love, and her heart ached at the thought.

"Arja? Did you hear me?" Camille asked, and Arja nearly jumped.

"How could I not?" she muttered, swallowing hard as she tried to cover for her inattention. "You are very loud."

"It helps scare away those with no sense of adventure."

Arja smirked. "Well, then, you already know I won't be frightened by you."

"Camille! What is taking you so long? Don't you see the storm coming?"

Both of them turned to see Camille's trading partner, Ephraim, standing on the deck of the *Sea Serpent*.

Arja bit her lip as Ephraim began shouting at Camille in another language. She'd been hoping to only have to bargain with Camille.

Together, the two of them were the most profitable merchants in Kyvan. While Camille was dark and largely built, Ephraim was shorter than Arja. His ruddy skin and a thin physique belied his sharp wit and clever mind.

A reluctant smile formed on her face as Camille argued back with Ephraim. She didn't know the language they were speaking, but she knew enough to know that Camille was explaining she wanted to purchase passage to Eydis. She could only hope Camille would make a good case for her. Ephraim was a hard negotiator, enough so that Arja knew she wasn't the only one who preferred Camille. Ephraim likely used his soft-hearted companion as a lure for more buyers. The two men made an excellent team despite their differences.

The only thing they appeared to have in common was the dragon tattoo on their forearms. She caught sight of Ephraim's tattoo as he began shaking his fist at Camille, who only shrugged.

"What is it?" Arja asked.

Finally, Ephraim looked at Arja, squinting his eyes at her.

"The price to go to Eydis costs more than coins," he warned her. "You should forget your quest and go back home."

"I won't." Arja stood her ground. "I've already told Camille. You can get some more money from me for my passage, or I'll find another way to the island."

Ephraim's wrinkled scowl deepened. "You don't understand."

"Does this mean you'll refuse my money?" Arja asked.

"He means well, my friend." Camille stepped in between them. "He is worried for your protection.

Eydis is a beautiful place, but there is much danger."

"You mean from the dragon?" Arja scoffed. "He doesn't come out unless it's dark. I should be safe enough during the daylight."

"While you are right, it is not wise to disregard such a force," Camille warned her lightly. "That is the very reason Ephraim doesn't want to let you come. You don't respect the forces at work in this world."

"Someone I know died on Eydis."

Camille held up his hands in a sympathetic gesture. "I'm sorry for your loss, but don't you think it's better not to lose anything more?"

"That's the reason I know I have to go," Arja said. "You say I don't respect Eydis' power. But the truth is, I fear it, Camille. My brothers are suffering, and if I don't do something, they'll die."

"How do you know this?"

Arja did not want to admit to her own nightmares and her heartbroken guilt over Sterlig's fate. She shrugged off the question.

"I have my ways. Perhaps I consulted a *seidr*," she said. "Would you believe me then?"

All the light and concern left Camille's eyes. "A lady with a power to command the demons is no one to dismiss," he said somberly.

Arja held back a grin. She enjoyed finding a way to use Camille's weaknesses, especially since

THE LEGEND OF EYDIS

he was so quick to seek out hers. "I need to go to the island so I can make peace with Sterlig's death. For my brothers' sakes as much as my own."

"Why are they not coming with you, too, then?" Camille asked, arching his brow as he glanced down at her. "Perhaps Ephraim and I would feel more inclined to let you aboard if we knew we could protect you better."

Arja was just about to assure Camille that she didn't need anyone to protect her when she heard a new voice call out her name.

"Arja!"

Arja felt her face turn red with anger and embarrassment as she saw Bjorn heading toward her. She briefly noticed Finnar was behind him before Bjorn blocked him from her view.

Why does he have to be here? Arja put her hands on her hips, bracing herself for another fight with Bjorn.

"Arja." Bjorn reached out, grabbing her arm as he nodded to Camille. "Excuse us, sir. I have to talk to her."

Camille bowed back graciously to Bjorn, clearly amused by Arja's expression. "Always a pleasure getting to speak with you, young Arja."

"We're not done negotiating," Arja said, elbowing Bjorn in the stomach before he could object.

Camille walked away, clearly holding back a fit of laughter.

The instant he was out of earshot, Arja ripped her wrist out of Bjorn's grasp.

"What are you doing here?" Arja snapped.

He held firm. "You're not going to Eydis."

"That's what you think." Arja crossed her arms over her chest. "You're not going to stop me."

"That's what you think." Bjorn's voice was full of mocking impatience as he grabbed her and pulled her back away from the ship. She dug in her heels, but he was too strong. Finnar's earlier taunting raced through her mind, and she thought of how Bjorn had always allowed her to win so he didn't have to hurt her. Her temper flared, increasing her determination not to lose this battle with him— whether or not he let her.

"I see my brothers managed to find you," she huffed. "You didn't need to bother coming for me."

"Apparently I did," Bjorn replied, still dragging her. "Why are you doing this, Arja?"

"Something needed to be done," Arja snapped, reaching for Bjorn's sword, the one she had buckled to her belt under her cloak. "You didn't want to help, so I'll do it by myself."

"What is your plan?" Bjorn looked her up and down. "I know you're one of the best shieldmaidens in Kyvan, but do you really think you can take on the dragon of Eydis?"

"What else can I do, Bjorn? This is a matter of honor." She shook her head. "And it's not like I have anywhere else to go."

"I understand how you feel right now, believe me." Bjorn looked away, and that was when Arja caught sight of his arm. There was a small pad around the area where she'd cut him earlier, and at that, Arja stopped trying to reach her sword.

She would still win against Bjorn, but she wasn't going to hurt him again.

"What about Jon? And Finnar?" She gestured back to where her brother had been only a moment before.

Finnar was still there, staring past Arja and Bjorn. His eyes were red and glazed over, while he wore an ashen expression on his face. Even from where she was standing, Arja could see he was trembling.

"Bjorn, look at him," she suddenly hissed. "Something is wrong."

Bjorn stopped dragging her back from the docks as he caught sight of Finnar.

"Finn?" he called, but Finnar didn't answer. Bjorn was about to go see him when Arja wrapped her fingers around his.

Arja could see the concern on his face, and she thought back to how insistent Finnar had been when he told her Bjorn wanted to protect her. As she looked from her brother to her friend, she felt hope stir inside of her again.

"Come with me, Bjorn."

Bjorn shook his head. "Your brother wanted me to stop you from going, not join you."

"But you want to protect me, right?" Arja smiled, suddenly confident she could win the argument. "Well, I'm going to Eydis, and if you want to do the honorable thing, you'll come with me."

"By the Allfather, Arja." Bjorn frowned and his eyes darkened. "You're not being fair."

"Who said this was fair? It wasn't fair of Sterlig to leave us in this position, was it?" Arja threw up her hands in exasperation. "Just come with me, Bjorn. I know you—and I might not be fair about this, but it's the right thing to do."

Bjorn sighed. "Arja—"

"Please? Please, Bjorn?" Arja latched onto his arm. "We can do this together. I know we can."

Bjorn ran his hand through his hair again, clearly distraught. Arja kept her gaze on him steady, even as Bjorn looked to Finnar, and then back at the *Sea Serpent*, and then heavenward, clearly desperate to find something that would recuse him.

Arja saw his eyes darken the moment he knew he was caught—and she knew she'd won.

"All right," he agreed, defeated. "I can't believe I am agreeing to this, but I'll help you."

"Yes!" Arja couldn't stop her grin. She jumped into his arms excitedly, embracing him tightly. There was a small, bittersweet tug in her heart as he instinctively encircled her. As much as he angered her, Arja hadn't wanted to say goodbye to him—and she really was grateful she wouldn't have to face Eydis all by herself.

"But you have to promise me, we will do this together," Bjorn said. "That means we make decisions together."

"You have my word as a shieldmaiden of Kyvan," she promised, burrowing her head against his shoulder. Catching sight of his wounded arm again, she softened. "Thank you, Bjorn."

Before he could let her go, Arja reached up and tangled her hands in his hair, pulling his lips down to hers in a searing kiss.

<u>6</u>

❖   ❖   ❖

Bjorn instantly forgot about everything else as Arja kissed him. Her lips were soft and welcoming against his, and he was too surprised to find a way to pull free—and by the time he realized he should step back, he had absolutely no interest in doing so.

The sweetness of her pummeled through him, as it mixed with the barest hint of sea spray between them. Before he knew what he was doing, he began to kiss her back, slanting his mouth over hers, letting himself delight in the full taste of her.

Bjorn had dreamed of kissing Arja for so long, but the reality of it overwhelmed him. He pressed harder against her, unable to stop himself. He felt her fingers fist in his hair, and he suddenly wondered if she had wanted to kiss him as badly as he had wanted to kiss her.

Arja shuddered against him.

"Bjorn," Arja breathed, and hearing his name said in such a sensual murmur sent another rush of pure desire straight through him. His hands moved down her back before settling onto her hips.

A crackle of thunder roared in the distance, breaking through the spell of Arja's kiss. Bjorn blinked and looked down at her.

Her sea goddess eyes glittered with wonder as she met his gaze. Before he could say anything, she blushed and scrambled back from him, giving him a nervous smile as she hurriedly untangled herself from him.

"Well then, I guess I'll go tell Camille we're both going now."

"Perhaps I should tell Finn." Bjorn's tongue felt thick in his throat as he spoke. It didn't help when he glanced over and saw Finnar looking at them with a stunned expression on his face.

At least the fear in Finnar's eyes had receded somewhat, Bjorn thought with a small smile.

"Be sure to hurry," Arja said. "Camille and Ephraim will likely want to cast off soon."

Bjorn only nodded, still unable to think clearly. The skies began to darken, while Arja cheerfully bounced toward the ship, more eager than ever to take care of their travel arrangements and acting as though she hadn't just kissed him passionately in the middle of the port.

What have I gotten myself into?

Regret stirred inside of him. Arja almost never said please, and it was foolish of him to think of giving into her when she put on her pretty manners.

A bolt of lightning struck out from the darkening sky as Bjorn made his way over to Finnar.

"After that, I assume you've agreed to take her?" Finnar asked. "Or is it my sister who's doing the taking?"

"What?" Bjorn blinked, confused. "What are you talking about?"

"Either way, it's good of you to marry Arja."

"I didn't—"

Amused, Finnar nudged him. "Come on, Bjorn. You know you've wanted her, and even I think Arja could do worse. But she's staying, and that's all that matters."

"No." Bjorn took hold of Finnar's shoulders. "I'm sorry, Finn. She wants to go. And if it'll give her peace over Sterlig's death, I at least owe her that, don't I?"

Finnar gaped at him. "But how are you going to slay the dragon? Even Sterlig couldn't do that!"

"We won't. We'll go to the island and find another way to honor Sterlig and allow Arja to make peace with his death."

"This is madness, Bjorn," Finnar said. "You're not thinking straight."

"Don't I know that," Bjorn murmured, glancing back at Arja, who was already standing with the sailor again, clearly enjoying another round of haggling.

"It's a three-day sojourn. Even with the good wind behind the sails. And it looks like rain."

"I won't leave Arja," Bjorn promised. "And I'll protect her, no matter what."

"Bjorn!" Arja called to him, waving her arm. "Let's go."

"Coming," Bjorn hollered back. He was about to ask Finnar if he would be all right while they were gone when he saw his sword on Arja's belt.

The pommel's eagle glimmered green, despite the dark clouds in the sky.

A sudden thought came to his mind.

Was it possible it was his sword which brought on his dreams? Finnar and Jon both had nightmares, too.

But then, why would Arja have any nightmares? She hadn't been with the sword at all, other than when Finnar and Jon had returned to their house, and there were others there, such as their many younger brothers, who would have suffered the same fate if that had been the cause.

"Do you see that?" Bjorn nudged Finnar. "Arja took my sword earlier, and—Finn?"

Finnar did not reply; he did not seem to be listening, either. Instead, he stared straight ahead. Bjorn followed his gaze, but there was nothing there.

"What is it? Finn?"

Finnar's blue eyes suddenly gleamed with a scarlet shadow. His expression went slack.

"Finn?" Bjorn clapped Finnar on the shoulder, but Finnar shrugged him off. "I know you're upset, but you know how Arja is … "

Bjorn repeated his promise that he would look after his sister, but Finnar said nothing. He only stared off into the clouds.

And then his body started shaking.

"Bjorn, come on!" Arja yelled. "I could use some help haggling here."

Bjorn looked back at Finnar and sighed. "I am sorry about this. Please take care of yourself while we're gone."

Finnar continued to say nothing, and Bjorn walked over towards Arja, confused by Finnar's silence. Normally his friend was always quick with a comeback, even when he was angry.

Bjorn came up beside Arja, who was still in the middle of their travel arrangements.

"I told you I wanted passage to Eydis." Arja pointed her finger at Camille, prodding him in the chest. "I didn't tell you for how many."

Camille's smiled faded. "That's not very honorable of you. This is twice as many people as you said before. Do I need to get Ephraim out here?"

"That just means you're close to surrender," Arja said. "Finish the deal, Camille. It's not very honorable if you don't uphold your end of the agreement, either."

"Arja, be fair," Bjorn said. He reached into his pack and pulled out his mother's crucifix. He hated the thought of what he was using it for, but he knew his mother would approve of using it for Arja's sake.

"Here," he said, holding it out to Camille. "This should take care of the price."

"Oh, my." Camille looked over at him with gratitude. "I like your husband, Arja."

Bjorn nearly choked, but Arja brightened and swiftly nodded. "Yes, yes, it's good to know he's good for something," she agreed quickly.

"Arja," Bjorn objected.

"There's no need to be embarrassed," Camille said, nodding back toward the port. "I saw you together over there."

"But—"

"Excuse us." Arja grabbed Bjorn and pulled him off to the side. "Bjorn, just let him think what he wants to think. We might get more out of our bargain if he thinks we're married. And that will help protect me from the other men on the ship. Do you want me subjected to their attentions all the way to Eydis?"

Bjorn glanced over at the ship, looking at the dozen of men sitting down next to their rowing stations. Many of them were burly men, strong after years of rowing through the seas between Eydis and Snæland.

"What were you going to do if I wasn't here?" he whispered back, suddenly curious of Arja's exact plans. It seemed like she had left a lot of room for error, and when she just shrugged, Bjorn felt like shaking her.

How could she make her plans like this? Hasn't she thought everything through?

Behind them, Camille cleared his throat. "Are we agreed to the final price, then?"

Bjorn nodded and held out his mother's gift.

"Stop." Arja stepped between his hand and Camille just as the rugged sailor was about to grab it. "There's no need to give Camille that, my, uh, dear husband. He's already agreed to the price before."

"It's all right, Arja," Bjorn said.

"No, it's not."

"Stop arguing with me." Bjorn scowled down at her, angry she'd already forgotten they were to work together. "This is a matter of honor."

She narrowed her eyes at him. "Camille's honor, not yours."

"That's enough." Camille pouted as he pushed Bjorn's hand aside. "Your bride is a cheat, good sir, and I will consider your passage to Eydis paid, thanks to my sympathy for you and her brothers."

"I am *not* a cheat," Arja objected.

"A cheat and a liar," Camille said, giving her a sharp but playful look.

Arja stepped back at his light chastisement, and at the shocked look on her face, Bjorn stepped in front of her protectively. "I'll happily defend my wife's honor."

"Happily, but foolishly." Camille snorted. He turned around. "I'd better tell Ephraim. Come along."

"We'll be there shortly," Bjorn said, as he took hold of Arja's hand and held her back. Once Camille was out of earshot, he rounded on her.

"You said you would work with me," Bjorn hissed.

"Well, I did, didn't I?" Arja put her hands on her hips. "You don't have to give him your mother's cross, Bjorn. I know what it means to you."

"Arja, that's not—"

"Not what? Fair? All is fair when it comes to haggling." Arja brushed her hair over her shoulder, indignant. "I got us a good price, Bjorn, and I know the vendor. Camille's soft, once you get under his skin."

"You've already forgotten your promise to me." Bjorn shook his head. "I told you that if we're going to Eydis, we're going to need to make plans together. This won't work if I can't trust you."

Arja took another step back, and then reached up and let her fingers lightly stroke the stubble on his chin. Bjorn hated how he stilled against her touch; he wondered if she had kissed him only so he would agree to her scheme.

"Of course you can trust me." Arja gave him a cheeky smirk. "I'm your wife, remember?"

"That's another thing I don't think—"

There was an ominous splash at the edge of the dock, followed by several cries. Bjorn and Arja turned to see the commotion.

"What happened?" Arja craned her neck to get a better look. There were a few sailors aboard the *Sea Serpent* tossing ropes into the water.

"It looks as though someone fell into the water." Bjorn saw the sword at her side again. It was glowing again.

A chill ran down his body.

He looked back over to where Finnar had been only a moment before, only to see his friend was gone.

"Arja, come with me." He took hold of her hand and pulled her into a run as he headed for the edge of the dock.

"What is it, Bjorn?" Arja stumbled, but Bjorn caught and steadied her. He said nothing as he watched a small group of men hoist a body out of the water.

At the sight of Finnar's familiar flop of dark hair, Arja gasped. She broke free from Bjorn and nudged her way through the men.

"Finnar." She grabbed hold of Finnar, helping him to his knees. He slushed out a mouthful of water and coughed.

"What happened?" Arja asked, looking at the surrounding sailors. "Finn?"

"Arja." Finnar let out a sad murmur as he slumped over, shaking violently as he leaned against her shoulder.

"So, I suppose we have another passenger now?"

Bjorn flinched at Camille's sudden reappearance. He'd missed the larger man's approach while he watched Finnar's rescue.

"What makes you say so?" Bjorn asked.

"He seems pretty determined to go," Camille said. "Wouldn't you say so, Arja?"

Arja was clearly shaken, but Bjorn's admiration for her swelled when she nodded firmly. "Yes," she agreed. "My brother will be coming with us."

"Good." Camille nodded and led the rest of the sailors away. "We'll be leaving shortly."

Bjorn came over and helped Finnar stand up. He was still shaking as Bjorn did his best to steady him.

"Are you sure you want to come with us?" Bjorn whispered. "I know you're afraid."

"I don't think I will live if I stay here." Finnar's voice was scratchy, and his eyes were lit with a reddish glow. He lowered his voice so only Bjorn could hear him. "I can't explain this feeling I have, Bjorn. I don't know how I ended up in the sea."

"But—"

"What did you think you were doing?" Arja whispered, cutting in on their conversation. "By the gods, it's been barely a week since Jon tried to do this, too."

"We're fortunate Finn was closer to the shore." Bjorn looked back at the other sailors, the ones who had rescued Finnar. It was good they had been there to help, too. "I'm not sure bringing him along is a good idea."

"We have no choice now." Arja wrapped her arm under Finnar's shoulder, letting him lean on her. "We need to make sure he's safe."

"We actually do have a choice. Bringing him along could put the rest of us in danger, too." Bjorn turned to Finnar. "I mean you no ill will, but will you be able to stop yourself from seeking death if you come to Eydis with us?"

"I survived Sterlig's visit." Finnar shook his head. He glanced at Arja. "And I should be doing this, too. Bjorn isn't the one you should've tricked into going to Eydis."

Arja bit her lip, but Bjorn shook his head.

"It's all right." Bjorn shrugged. "My father has disowned me. I am not welcome at my home. It seems that I was meant to go on this journey."

"What?" Arja's mouth dropped open at his confession, but before she could say anything, he shook his head.

What else could he say? Bjorn wondered. From arguing with Arja earlier, and then fighting with his father, and now about to embark on a journey to help his friends, it had been a long day, and it was far from over.

He looked over at Arja, remembering their kiss and how much he'd always loved her. While he worried for his mother, and abhorred the thought of becoming Sterlig's replacement, he was certain of his desire to protect Arja.

"We need to go," Bjorn said. "The ship is casting off. We will make our plans once we get on board."

Finnar and Arja nodded, and Bjorn nodded, relieved Arja was finally willing to work with him.

As they turned to board the *Sea Serpent*, he caught sight of his sword again.

He caught her by the arm. "Arja."

"What is it?"

"I think it's best if I get my sword back," Bjorn said quietly. He held out his hand expectantly.

Arja grimaced, but she dutifully unbuckled the sword and handed it to him. After that, she ran to catch up with Finnar and Camille.

Bjorn tied the sword to his belt. When he was done, he felt better. The sword must be connected to

Sterlig's death and the nightmares that haunted them, and Bjorn was glad it was away from Arja.

As he headed up the gangway plank, he grabbed hold of the pouch on the other side of his belt, the one that held his mother's gift. As he boarded the ship, he closed his eyes and prayed for the comfort and strength to see this journey through.

He opened his eyes again, just in time to see lightning strike down in the distance, the light stabbing the sea as the stormy skies only grew darker.

It was not a good sign, he thought.

THE LEGEND OF EYDIS

7

◇   ◇   ◇

The *Sea Serpent* left port, pushing against the raging water. As Arja helped Finnar settle into the ship's hold with the cargo, Bjorn walked toward the prow, studying the stormy horizon.

Soon he would see Eydis, the island from his nightmares, and there he would find a way to help Arja make peace with Sterlig's death; maybe in doing so, his own father's longing for honor would be satisfied.

All he had to do was survive.

"Watch out, would you?"

Bjorn quickly stepped aside as Ephraim, carrying a large barrel, brushed past him and headed toward the stern.

Bjorn followed after him. "Are you certain we should be sailing in this weather?"

"What's there to be certain of?" Ephraim scoffed. "This is what we do. This is what we have always done. Three days at sea, two days at port, and then we get a few days of rest once we arrive home."

When Arja had introduced them earlier, Bjorn had recognized the small, squat little man as a dedicated merchant and businessman. From the lines at his eyes and the deep frown lines on his brow and cheeks, Bjorn could tell he was a seasoned one, as well. Ephraim and Camille argued with each other as they organized their rowers and help set the sail. Watching them, Bjorn could appreciate Camille for his obvious pleasure at frivolity, just as he could agree with Ephraim for his frugality.

"This is not ideal," Ephraim muttered as he pushed another crate to the side. The little man tutted his tongue and scowled before he glanced down at the dragon tattoo on his forearm. "But we will go. We have no choice, not after lingering this long."

"I apologize if Arja delayed your journey," Bjorn said. "I didn't realize her bargaining took so long."

"It wasn't that," Ephraim scoffed. "But don't remind me of her. Camille should've made you pay more for the trouble of going out in this storm. If her father wasn't such a good customer, I'd toss her overboard without a second thought. Now, make yourself useful and secure the backstay. My men are busy rowing."

Bjorn hid a smile. There were downsides to dealing with good customers; he knew that from his own experiences in the Kyvan marketplace.

As he rushed to help secure the sail, the boat lurched dangerously.

Bjorn grabbed hold of Ephraim to stop him from falling, but he only bristled. "Thank you, but there's no need for you to do that. Once you're done with the backstay, you'd better get below deck."

"Why do you have such a strict schedule? Are there no exceptions?"

There was a long pause as Ephraim pushed the heavy crate further into the stern. In the distance, lightning struck and thunder roared, and Bjorn could see the rain as it poured down from the clouds.

"It's not something you should concern yourself with," Ephraim finally said. "But generally, I can say we are under contract with the Princess Brynja and we must keep to the schedule. Our time is running out."

Ephraim glanced back at the clouds and shook his head. Then he cupped his hands over his mouth and called out for his trading partner. "Camille!"

"Casting off." Camille heaved a big groan as he kicked off the wharf and jumped into the knarr. He settled in with a practiced ease, and then he let out a loud chuckle. "There we go. We'll be fine now."

Ephraim scoffed. "That's what you think. We're still carrying passengers. The princess won't be pleased."

"She isn't in charge of the weather," Bjorn said. "I'm sure—"

THE LEGEND OF EYDIS

The stormy skies lit up with forks of lightning colored red and gleaming with supernatural fury. Bjorn went silent, staring up into the rain in fearful wonder.

"What are you so sure of now?" Ephraim huffed. He walked over to Camille and smacked his head. "You see? This is not good."

"Calm down, my friend," Camille replied. "We will be fine."

"That remains to be seen. Look!"

Bjorn watched as Ephraim stuck his arm in front of Camille's face. From where he was standing, Bjorn could see the tattoo was glowing with an angry red.

He felt his mouth drop open, even as Camille laughed and put his large arm around Ephraim's thin shoulders.

"We will be fine," Camille repeated, his voice much more uncharacteristically hard this time. "You worry too much."

"Only because you don't worry enough!"

"If I worried as much as you do, you would still say I didn't worry enough," Camille said. "So I don't worry at all."

"You still lie plenty." Ephraim slipped out of Camille's reach.

"Of course I do." Camille turned to give Bjorn a wink. "But that's a large part of not worrying. The other part is not thinking."

Bjorn gave the sailor a rueful smirk. He was going to ask about their tattoos when Arja called out to him.

"Bjorn." Arja waved from the top of the small staircase leading down into the hold. "Come settle in."

"I'll be right there," Bjorn said. "I just want to talk to Camille for a moment."

Camille patted his shoulder. "You might want to ask me your question, but it's better if you go prepare your quarters. Your wife will likely need you. Women like to keep order, and the *Sea Serpent* is hardly a place to call home, especially in a storm."

"But—"

"And for any other questions you may or may not have," Camille said with a pointed look, "it's better if you ask when we eat. Tongues roll a little more loosely when we're consuming the mead and eating through our rations."

Bjorn slowly nodded. There was a time for questions, but this was clearly not it—not when they were facing a storm. It was best for him to get out of the crew's way.

Besides, being with Arja and Finnar would allow them to plan for Eydis.

He made his way down to the hold, just as he felt the first drops of rain.

And then he heard Finnar and Arja arguing.

"I can't stop this. It's a curse, I swear," Finnar yelled.

"Curse or not, you have to control yourself," Arja argued back. "How hard is it to stay put?"

"You don't know what it's like."

"I've had the nightmares, too!" Arja threw up her hands. "I've seen Sterlig die, but I'm not eager to die like you are."

Finnar scowled. "What do you mean, you've had nightmares, too? You never said so."

"She told me." Bjorn cleared his throat and stepped between them. He dropped his pack and then looked back and forth between the two of them. "That's why I'm here."

"Wait." Finnar narrowed his eyes at Arja. "So, you're not really doing this for me, are you? You're doing this for yourself."

"I am not."

"Yes, you are," Finnar insisted. "And now you've manipulated Bjorn and me into coming, too."

"I didn't want you to come. You're the one who tried to kill himself and now we have to watch you since you can't seem to stop yourself." Arja shifted uncomfortably. "I can only hope Mother will make sure Jon doesn't do this while we're gone."

"Can you two please calm down? What's done is done," Bjorn said.

"Yes, Arja, listen to your *husband*," Finnar taunted.

Arja lunged at her brother, but Bjorn hurried forward and caught her. He wrapped his arms around her, holding her fast as the boat continued to rock. Above Arja's hollered threats, Bjorn could hear the rowers calling out orders while their oars pushed through the sea.

When Arja threatened to do something particularly vicious to Finnar's manhood, however, Bjorn cleared his throat loudly.

"Stop, Arja."

Arja turned her rage against him, glaring over her shoulder. "Fast enough when it suits you, aren't you?"

"Finn came to help us," Bjorn said.

"That's a lie."

"I'd just as soon as save Finn from your wrath. He'll be able to help me protect you later."

"I don't need your protection." Arja finally wriggled free from Bjorn. "I came for other reasons."

"No, you didn't. You came for yourself. And for Sterlig, too," Finnar reminded her. "Your beloved, right?"

As Arja clenched her fists, Bjorn bit back a sigh and decided it was best to redirect their attention before another fight ensued. They would be landing on Eydis in three days' time, and there was no way to turn back now.

"We're going to have to work together while we're here," Bjorn said. "That means we need a plan."

"She doesn't have one," Finnar said.

Arja scowled at him. "I don't need an exact plan."

"We should have an idea of what to do when we get to Eydis." Bjorn had to remind himself not to roll his eyes at Arja's irresponsibility. "Even Sterlig wouldn't have just decided to go."

"I guess you don't know your brother as well as you think," Finnar said with a sour laugh. "He didn't have much of a plan either, past stealing your father's knarr and taking me and some of the thralls."

Bjorn frowned. "He didn't have a plan?"

"Sterlig imagined himself quite the hero," Finnar said. "He thought he could get to Eydis and slay the dragon, just as he could easily have raided and pillaged the place. That was his plan, and he altered it at every turn."

Bjorn and Arja exchanged worried looks, then Arja looked away in shame.

Bjorn watched her carefully, unsure of what to do. She had come to save her brothers—and yes, probably herself to a small degree. If she also came to avenge Sterlig, it likely hurt to be reminded of his fate. Now that they were supposedly married for the sake of their trip, Bjorn knew he could easily remind her of what she'd lost.

The ship jostled forward, and Bjorn caught Arja's arm in one hand and the mast in the other. As Finnar took hold of another nearby post, Bjorn pulled Arja close to him.

"Careful," he whispered.

From the look on her face, Arja was likely going to argue with him. But then another wave crashed into the starboard side of the ship, and Arja's grip tightened around him.

Just as the keel leveled, another sailor stumbled down the stairs from the top deck.

"We need your help," he said, gripping the handrailing as another wave slammed into the ship. "The ship's taking on water. We need all the help we can get."

"Tell me what you need," Finnar said. He let go of his post and pushed himself toward the stairs, falling into them as another wave rocked the ship. "I'm tired of the company down here."

"No, Finn." Bjorn tucked Arja's hand around the mast. "Both of you stay here. I'll go help."

"Let me go, too," Arja said, grabbing his tunic. "I can help."

"Arja, please … " She was a year younger than he was, but it felt more like a lifetime at times like these. He glanced down at her, ready to be firm and fair—but then another wave tossed across the ship, and he fell forward, pinning Arja between himself and the mast.

He was about to apologize, even though she would see him as weak, when he caught sight of her lips.

She was flustered and angry, and always arguing, and all Bjorn could think of in that moment was how she melted against him earlier when she'd kissed him. Everything in that moment had hinted at how she could be sweet and pliant despite her stubbornness.

Just like his metalwork, all he needed was a little heat between them.

"We're clearly in trouble," Arja said. "Name one reason I shouldn't help."

In reply, Bjorn leaned down and kissed her again. Another wave tumbled through him, but he couldn't be sure of whether it was the shock of their kiss or the storm outside the boat. No matter what it was, he was happy to fall against Arja, pressing into her as she went still. He fit his mouth to hers, softening their embrace ever so slightly as he tasted her.

Her fingers, still fastened on his tunic, tightened and tugged him closer.

It was the smallest movement of her surrender, and he relished in it.

But triumph was short-lived; as much as his heart wanted the rest of the world to fall away, the sea was demanding his attention. The chill of rainwater drenched his boots, as the rain slid below deck and pooled at their feet.

Abruptly, he jerked himself away from Arja, desperately trying to keep his emotions hidden as he met her gaze.

"Stay here," he ordered. "The other men need to see me protecting you. You're my wife, remember?"

Arja was silent with shock as Bjorn let her go. With her lips slightly parted and her eyes wide, it was the first time Bjorn had ever seen her stunned speechless.

He held onto the picture she made as he left her below deck. He didn't have need to hear the various commands Camille was shouting out to know he was walking into chaos.

THE LEGEND OF EYDIS

8

"Watch out!"

Bjorn arrived on the deck just as the buntline snapped. He ducked his head just as the rope whipped by, and when he righted himself, he found Ephraim glaring at him.

"I'm fine," Bjorn assured him.

"The rest of us aren't," Ephraim snapped. "This wouldn't be happening if you and your family had the good sense to stay at Kyvan."

"You can hardly blame us for the weather."

Ephraim's scowl deepened, and then he moved away.

"So much for trying to be friendly."

"Ephraim prefers people who are useful," Camille said from behind him.

"He's not the only one who feels that way," Bjorn muttered, his hopes deflated as Camille handed him the snapped rope.

"Here. Secure the buntline again. Tie it down and help the tiller keep the rudder steady." Camille pointed to a burly sailor at the stern of the ship.

"All right." Bjorn nodded. "And that'll make it better?"

"The ship, yes; Ephraim, no. But don't worry. I'm sure I can convince him of how useful you and your family are yet, and that will make dealing with him easier."

"Thank you, but truth be told, I'm more useful as a blacksmith."

"You're plenty useful then. Smithing requires strength, focus, and endurance, and if you've got all of that, it's a good start to learning how to sail." Camille grunted as another wave butted against the ship and splashed over onto the deck.

Bjorn hurried to retie the buntline, just as the ship cut through a large wave. The spray was fierce, dousing his clothes and knocking him back onto the deck, but Bjorn stood back up and pressed harder against the rudder.

"Keep rowing, men," Camille called. "No time to heave-ho today. Pull up the sails and secure them!"

Lightning scorched the skies, flickering like a ghost along the heavy clouds.

"Bjorn."

Bjorn went still. There was a whisper on the wind. Someone was calling his name.

"Sterlig?" Bjorn whispered, and then shook his head, trying to clear the rain and mist out of his face. He struggled to keep the rudder steady, even as another wave pummeled against the ship.

"Bjorn."

There was no mistaking it this time. Bjorn stood up quickly, not even noticing as his feet rocked against the hard wood of the ship as the waves began to diminish.

Bjorn felt his palms suddenly drip with sweat as he pulled out his sword. It was glowing again; its greenish tint lit up along the blade, its intensity deepening inside the ruts of the runic inscription.

"You don't even feel bad that I've died, do you? You wretched brother! How can you avenge me?"

His heart thundered in his chest as he heard Sterlig's condemnation give voice to his heart's most hidden secret.

"Bjorn."

Camille's voice cut through the storm inside of Bjorn, and he blinked. He found himself standing on the deck of the *Sea Serpent*, his sword tight in his hand as he stood ready to fight.

Flustered, Bjorn stumbled as the boat shifted, while water dripped down from his hair. "What happened?"

"What happened indeed?" Camille peered at him through the drizzling rain. "You look like you've seen a ghost."

Bjorn shook his head, slowly putting his sword away; it no longer glowed. He didn't know what happened, and he didn't know if he wanted to.

Was it possible he'd heard a ghost speak to him? Was it really Sterlig?

And what if he was right about me?

"Men are meant to navigate storms, both the ones we face on the seas and the ones we bear inside ourselves," Camille told him. "Truth is the morning star that guides us, and we find fresh reserves of honor when we pull into peaceful harbors."

"Assuming we survive." Bjorn looked down at his sword glumly.

"Of course we will survive our storms, Bjorn. We have to, or we cease to live. That is how when we fight, we know we win even if we die."

For the first time, Bjorn noticed the storm had let up slightly, enough so that the boat was stable and the waves, while still rolling against them with ferocity, were more manageable.

"Here." Camille handed him a pail. "Start hauling water. I can manage the till."

Bjorn saw the deck was overrun with scattered puddles of seawater. His clothes were soaked, and the wind was still blowing. He pulled off his tunic, irritated by the slogging feel of the fabric against his skin. As he began to work, he hoped Arja was safe and comfortable below deck.

❖   ❖   ❖

Between the rain and thunder and the roaring waves, even under the ship's deck Arja had plenty to distract her. She secured several barrels worth of

114

ale and freshwater toward the bow and stacked up a large fishing net in the back of the hold, hoping it would be easy to use as a makeshift sleeping pallet during the night. As if to test her theories, Finnar leaned back and closed his eyes to rest. Arja allowed him to do so, glad that he wasn't fighting his way off the ship.

Chores were a helpful distraction. The last thing she wanted was to find herself turning idle, staring out into nothingness as she thought of Bjorn, reliving that moment when he'd taken hold of her and claimed her mouth with his own.

Arja traced her lips with her fingers, closing her eyes as she thought of his kiss. He tasted like fire and forest, of adventure—and in that moment, the combination of his recklessness and his deliberateness had left her breathless.

All of that warmth disappeared at the reminder he'd given her about their charade. He'd used it as a way to manipulate her—as he no doubt thought she'd done to him before—and he'd succeeded.

Arja glanced around; the work she'd done was hardly noticeable. Above her, the men were still calling out orders, though the intensity of the sea had lightened some.

"You're my wife, remember?"

Bjorn's choice of words burned into her; she wasn't the one who had trouble with commitment, even if their current arrangement required maintaining a falsehood.

Arja pursed her lips as she played with the fishing net, and then she smiled. If Bjorn was going to use her own trickery against her, she would make sure he paid dearly for it.

Finnar shifted in the large net pile. "I don't think you're being fair to Bjorn, you know."

"He told me that he's had the nightmares, too," Arja said. "It's only logical that he would come with me to Eydis. You're the one who's not supposed to be here."

"I didn't mean that. You shouldn't be pretending you're married to him."

"It's for my protection."

"I can understand where it might save you from their attentions, but it's not going to stop the men from asking you to prepare their dinner." Finnar gave her a taunting smirk. "Besides, you're still using him for your pleasure more than your protection."

Arja blushed and turned away. "I don't know what you're talking about."

"Yes, you do. Bjorn's an honorable man. You shouldn't be teasing him like this." He sighed. "I don't understand the necessity of this illusion. Why not just let him marry you for real?"

"Bjorn's already told me he doesn't want to marry me, that's why," Arja snapped. "If you *must* know."

Finnar went quiet. Arja felt the same earlier stab of humiliation, admitting Bjorn had rejected her. She cleared her throat, determined to hide her pain.

"We'd already talked about it earlier this morning and he said no. But then Camille thought we were married after I kissed him on the dock, so I went along with it for the sake of convenience. And the added benefit of protection, as I said earlier."

She went back to work, organizing the barrels of water and mead on the other side of the hold. When she came back, Finnar sat up.

Arja steeled herself for his questions.

"So you asked him to marry you earlier?" Finnar said.

Arja sighed. "Do you have to bother me about this?"

"I was with him earlier. I'm the one who told him to come and get you. He didn't say anything about seeing you this morning."

"Bjorn is an honorable man, remember?" Arja huffed indignantly. "He wouldn't have wanted you to think he was insulting me. Or he didn't want to have to deal with you over the matter."

"Yes, that's all true, but it's very unlikely that he would turn you down if you wanted to marry him."

Arja stiffened. She knew that Bjorn had wanted to kiss her that morning in the forge, and she could easily relive the moment when he kissed her back.

"That's not how you presented the idea to Bjorn before, was it?" Finnar arched his brow at her. "That marrying you was a convenient idea because you could use your dowry to pay for his family's debts? And that it might help me and Jon with our cursed nightmares?"

"No, of course not." Arja crossed her arms. "I mean, not exactly."

"You didn't tell him he should marry you because Sterlig was dead, did you?" Finnar frowned, but a moment later, he shook his head. "No, not even you would do that. Bjorn wouldn't be here if you insulted him that badly."

Arja's cheeks flushed over with crimson heat. She had mentioned that a few times when she'd talked with Bjorn. "How would that insult him? I mean, Sterlig is dead, and now I can get married. Bjorn seems like a logical choice, doesn't he?"

"By the gods, Arja." Finnar groaned, and then rolled back against the ship's hull and laughed. "That's what you said, wasn't it? I swear, I'll never understand you. First you agree to marry Sterlig, and after he dies, you assume his brother will be eager to replace him because of money."

"And your well-being," Arja added, which only made Finnar shake his head.

THE LEGEND OF EYDIS

"Bjorn is honorable, but first to those he loves," Finnar said. "At this rate, he probably only came to stop you from going to Eydis because I asked. And look where we are now."

"Are you trying to make me push you overboard?" Arja stormed over to him to glare down at him. "No one would be able to rescue you this time. Not this far from shore and in this weather."

"I would happily die, knowing you'd regret it."

"Well, then, if you're going to punish me in your death, it seems I was right to bring you along to Eydis and make sure you live."

"Sailing on a ship is punishment enough," Finnar agreed, putting his hands behind his head and leaning back. "I barely managed to sleep at all when Jon and I came with Sterlig. This time isn't going to be any different."

"Bjorn and I can toss you under the keelson," Arja said. "It's wet, but not enough for you to effectively drown yourself."

"The lapstrake area is fine," Finnar said, gesturing to the far side of the hold. "It might even offset the ship's rocking some. So even if I can't sleep, I'll be useful."

"I've got plenty of room for Bjorn to sleep with me over here on the nets," Arja said, just as Bjorn came down to the hold.

"Sleep with you?" Bjorn stumbled down the rest of the stairs, making Finnar laugh.

Arja forced herself not to blush at the sight of his bare chest. He'd taken off his tunic and tucked it around his waist, where it hung in limp, wet rags. The rain and seawater added a layer of slickness to the muscles of his chest and arms. Blacksmithing and the hours of pounding and shaping metal of all sorts had given Bjorn a sharp, defined look, and Arja found it difficult to focus on anything else.

"But we're not really together," Bjorn said.

"What?" Arja blinked and turned away, trying not to blush.

"We're not really together," Bjorn repeated.

"Oh." Arja swallowed and put on a teasing smile. "But aren't we, though, *maður*?"

She walked over and ruffled his hair, before locking her arm around his and letting her other hand run up his arm, ignoring how rigid his body went at her caress. She was enjoying the sensation of touching him when her hand ran into the bandage on his arm, and then Arja quickly pulled away in shame, especially when she saw his own expression shade over with discomfort.

"No," he said.

Finnar sighed. "I thought that was part of the plan. Just go along with it, Bjorn."

"We don't actually have a plan," Bjorn reminded him. "Remember?"

THE LEGEND OF EYDIS

"Nothing's wrong with the one we have so far," Arja said. "We'll get to Eydis, and go look for the dragon, slay it, and then go home."

"That's not a plan."

A small bell rang from above deck, and Arja turned her head at the sound of Camille's voice.

"Come and sup with us, my friends," Camille called. "The rain has stopped, and we are all hungry."

"Coming," Bjorn shouted back. He glanced at Arja and Finnar. "Time to eat. And this will be good for us to be with the others."

"Why?" she sneered. "So you can be seen 'protecting' your wife again?"

"What? No." Bjorn glared at her before he grabbed another tunic from his pack and pulled it over his head. "We need to get more information about Eydis, and this is our chance."

"What's there to know?" Arja huffed. "We know the legend."

"Not all legends are based in truth," Bjorn reminded her. "The fact that the story is legendary means it's likely too long since someone sat down and looked at the facts. Camille and the others can help us."

She sighed. "They're perfume traders, not dragon slayers."

"Arja." Bjorn took her arm. "I saw something when I was up there and we were leaving Kyvan. Camille and Ephraim both have the same tattoo."

"Some men get them," Arja said. "And women, too. Even Sterlig had a few of—"

"I know that. But no one I've ever met has had them glow—and the aura is not completely unfamiliar." Bjorn looked over at Finnar. "I've seen it before."

Arja sighed, moving back toward the fishing net and leaning against the wall.

Just this morning, she mused, she'd walked over to see Bjorn in his forge, and now she was pretending to be married to him while she was on a mission to avenge Sterlig's death and save her brothers from their nightmares.

Arja looked over at her brother. He was older than her by a summer or so, and he'd always been gracious to her. She had felt justified in coming aboard the *Sea Serpent*, hoping that her quest would be helpful to both Finnar and Jon.

What if I've only made things worse? Arja rubbed her arms, chilled at the thought.

She'd already caused all of this to happen. What if this was wrong after all?

As if he was thinking the same thing, Bjorn came up beside her. He let his hand fall on hers, a gesture that could've easily been pity as much as comfort.

"Trust me on this, Arja. We need a plan, but it's also clear we need more information. There's more to the story we know. Especially if we're going to have a plan for when we dock at Eydis."

Arja sighed. "Does this mean I have to cook?"

She was grateful when Bjorn laughed.

"Doubtful. The seafaring men have their dried fish. But Ephraim has mentioned there's some fruit and Camille is eager for his mead."

"You two should go." Finnar waved his arm, gesturing for them to leave. "I think it's better if I just stay down here."

"Why, Finn?" Arja arched her brow at him. "You've never refused a meal before. Not unless you were sick."

"Perhaps I am sick." Finnar shrugged, and then slumped over. "But I think it's better I don't get near the water. If Bjorn thinks the supernatural is at work in all of this, I'm better not taking any chances."

"I don't know if there's anything supernatural involved." Bjorn shifted uncomfortably. "But if there's a dragon on Eydis, we might as well consider it."

"The gods are cruel to us," Finnar said with a sigh.

"Perhaps they are not gods, so much as demons," Bjorn murmured, startling Arja.

"Do you think so?" she asked.

"I can't say. Not without more information. So, come," Bjorn squeezed his hand around hers and tugged her to follow after him. "They've been working hard all day to get us out of the storm. What better way for a beautiful goddess like yourself to make them feel appreciated than by giving them food and drink?"

"Excellent point," Arja said, brightening. She entwined her arms around Bjorn's neck. "I should thank you first and foremost, though, shouldn't I? Since you were my beloved husband, protecting me all this time?"

Bjorn chuckled nervously. "Come on, no one but Finnar is here," he said, trying to disengage himself from her embrace. "There's no need to—"

"Oh, there isn't?" Arja leaned upward, only a breath away from his lips. "Are you certain, Bjorn?"

She felt his body go tense with longing, but she never took her eyes off his. Without his tunic on, there was little to stop her from reveling in the tremor she felt between them. His eyes were brown, dotted with the smallest flecks of amber and jasper, and she could see the struggle he faced inside of him.

"I'm certain." Finnar snorted. "Save it for the real audience, you two."

Arja grinned. "You're going to have to play-act better than this, if you want to convince the others that I'm yours, Bjorn."

"Arja—"

"Come on." She shifted out of his arms, grabbing his hand as she headed up the stairs to the upper deck.

She'd wanted to retaliate for his kiss earlier, and it was intoxicating to be back in control when it came to managing Bjorn—no matter how closely she was to losing control herself.

THE LEGEND OF EYDIS

9

Camille had been right about the mead.

Bjorn watched the small crowd of sailors as they finally cracked a smile, enjoying the late night and the following drinks and food. Arja had found their rations and even served them graciously, putting on her best smile as she talked up some of the rowers. Bjorn was grateful she agreed with his plan of questioning the crew, but he was still careful to watch over her—or more accurately, he watched the men who talked with her. After the fear inspired by the storm, the men were all too eager to drink in her simple kindness and her goddess-given beauty. Bjorn heard them thank her in flirtatious ways, but Arja easily dismantled their comments without deflating their egos, using similar tactics when she was trading or buying in the marketplace. Most of the men gave up flirting with her as she turned their attention to Bjorn.

"I'm fortunate that I already have such a worthy husband," Arja said, with enough of an air Bjorn knew she was teasing him as much as dissuading them.

Bjorn could only smirk at her.

Even if she didn't love him the way she'd loved Sterlig, she was enjoying their charade. When he'd kissed her before, she had been clearly shocked he was willingly playing along, even if it was for her own good. Now she was over her surprise and using every chance she could to push back against him.

It was not too different from how she would fight him in their sword duels, Bjorn recalled. Arja would taunt him into striking before turning his attack's power back on him. When he won, it was usually because he could outlast her with patience.

"Still a bit of a liar and a cheat, but she's a comely one," Camille said as he came up behind him. He offered Bjorn a tankard, and Bjorn took it eagerly. It burned into him, igniting some of his spirit against the encroaching darkness. It had been more than two summers since he'd gone sailing, and he'd forgotten the air's taste of saltiness as much as the horizon's playful danger.

"I owe a round of thanks to you," Camille continued. "It's good to have an extra hand or two on deck when a storm brews. It doesn't happen very often."

Bjorn nodded at the tattoo on Camille's arm. "Because you have protection?"

Camille winked. "The worst sort, if you must know."

"So Ephraim was right earlier?" Bjorn watched as Camille ate some more dried fruit. The old man looked thoughtful, pausing as he weighed out his response.

THE LEGEND OF EYDIS

"You know the legend of Eydis," Camille said finally. "The dragon is very possessive of Princess Brynja. And that means the people on the island are bound to her, as well."

Bjorn tensed. "Was the storm actually our fault, then? Since we are not part of your contract?"

"No. It was mine," Camille said. "I'm not supposed to allow travelers on the ship. In a way, it was good of Arja to negotiate for such a cheap passage. I have a feeling there's a loophole big enough for my guests. Though perhaps it is a loophole attached to a noose."

"You're certainly risking a lot then." Bjorn frowned.

"Ah well, a deal's a deal, even with a treacherous dealer." Camille shrugged, and then he patted Bjorn on the shoulder and laughed. "You must have some idea of the same when it comes to your wife, right?"

"I will still defend my wife's honor," Bjorn said quietly. He did not like how Camille likened marriage to a deadly trade agreement, even though he knew there were others who did the same.

Camille quickly stopped laughing. "Aye, a besotted fool you are. And that's good for a husband, so I respect that. Excuse me. I'd best see to my men for the night. We get some relief at night, so we can watch the moon and map the stars."

THE LEGEND OF EYDIS

It appeared the weather was at the whim of the dragon, too.

Bjorn frowned. "Tell me, before you go, why does your tattoo glow?"

"You can see the glow, then?" Camille nodded prudently. "I was right about you, then. Good."

"Right about what?"

"If one is going to slay the dragon of Eydis, it takes a man of true honor," Camille explained. He held up his arm, giving Bjorn a closer look at the design on his arm. "All the men on my ship and all the residents of Eydis have the tattoo of the dragon."

Bjorn watched as the tattoo glowered at him, burning more brightly as he reached out his hand. Camille pulled back.

"It's best if you don't. It's made from her blood, and if you can truly see how much hatred you inspire in her spirit, you should keep your distance."

"Her?"

"Interesting how most warriors assume the dragon is a male, isn't it?" Camille's eyes glittered in momentary amusement, before darkening. "No, the dragon is a female, all right; both beautiful and terrible to behold, just like women themselves. Clever in ways men cannot anticipate, and ever more deadly when they have the upper hand."

Camille chuckled. "That's why it takes an honorable man to defeat the dragon, doesn't it?

Nothing slays a woman out for vengeance like a man who stands for justice. He does not deserve her ire, and she is furious at the thought of such a reality."

Vengeance? Bjorn frowned. The legend said the dragon of Eydis was there to protect Princess Brynja, not take vengeance for her.

Before Bjorn could ask another question, Camille yelped and gripped his arm.

Bjorn gasped as he saw the dragon tattoo flare into a deadly shine.

"Camille?" Arja came up beside them, holding a small box of dried fish. "What's wrong?"

"My apologies," he said through gritted teeth. He gave Bjorn a pained wink and added, "I've said too much for her liking. Excuse me."

Camille limped away, leaving Bjorn alone with Arja.

"What was that about?" Arja asked.

"He was telling me about the dragon," Bjorn said. "What have you found out?"

"Nothing new," Arja said with a sigh. She put down the box of food and picked at it. "But I haven't been able to ask a lot of questions since I've been busy playing mother to all these love-hungry sailors."

"You're sure you're not playing temptress?" Bjorn teased.

She scowled at him. "A sheep could be serving them dinner and they'd build an altar to worship it. Don't you dare make fun of me for this."

"I wasn't making fun—not of you, anyway, so much as with you. Or attempting to." Bjorn wrapped his arm around her shoulder and pulled her closer. "I would like to know if I need to fend off any unwanted admirers."

"Who says they're unwanted?" Arja arched her brow at him, giving him a taunting look.

"Me. I am your husband, after all." Bjorn grinned as he pulled her closer, forcing her to place her hand on his chest. He could see the fluster on her face, even in the moonlight. He was starting to enjoy Arja's game, especially since winning didn't require battling her with anything other than his wits. "And that's why it's best for you to let me hold you. The men can see how we love each other."

"Are you sure it's not too much of a burden?"

"If it's not one for you."

Arja shrugged, but Bjorn felt her lean against him. "I suppose it's fine—since we need to."

Bjorn hid a smile; it was good to know she enjoyed his attentions, just as it was good of him to put a stop to them. He was already deceiving the others onboard the *Sea Serpent*. There was no need to allow himself to be deceived by his own lies, too.

THE LEGEND OF EYDIS

Bjorn cleared his throat. "That's why we need to learn more about the dragon of Eydis and the rest of the island's history."

"Well, we already know the main part of it," Arja said. "Eydis broke away from the mainland when Prince Andor was killed in a battle. His spirit came to protect Princess Brynja in the form of a dragon, and ever since then, she and her small island of residents have lived there. They have a great treasure on Eydis, their perfume, and whoever can slay the dragon gets to marry the princess and take the treasure for his own."

"I was talking to Camille just now and he says that the dragon is a female," Bjorn said. "I doubt Prince Andor's spirit would be manifested in such a form."

"Why? Because men are stronger?" Arja asked, clearly skeptical.

"No, not because of that," Bjorn said. "It's more because of the way a man loves a woman. A man who is in love with a woman will do anything in the world to be with her, protect her, provide for her. There's a sense of responsibility that goes deeper than most thoughts, to the heart of all creation. Love like that is so real, it can't be contained by only two bodies any longer; being bound together allows for their spirit to procreate into something tangible, even if it's not visible. That ache is there, to fill the world with our love."

"Our love?" Arja's voice was soft as she took a step closer to him.

"Their love, I mean." Bjorn looked away in a hurry, hiding his sudden discomfort. He had allowed himself to get caught up in the moment, standing there with Arja.

He cleared his throat. "And so, a dragon taking away a chunk of land to create an island at their separation doesn't seem quite right, especially when it's a female. It's more of a defensive move."

"To protect the princess," Arja reminded him. "Makes perfect sense to me."

"It doesn't to me." Bjorn watched as she wrinkled her little nose. She finally relaxed against his arm, though she was still careful to avoid the injury she'd caused him, and the way she pressed her body against his body nearly made him confess everything to her. "If someone separated me from you, I wouldn't rest until they were dead," he said. "I wouldn't turn into a dragon to protect you. I'd turn into a dragon to kill them for robbing me of you."

Their eyes met, and hers twinkled with starlight and seawater. Slowly, her gaze fell to his lips, and Bjorn stood still as he waited for her decision.

And then she jerked away, looking across the deck.

Bjorn scratched his head and blushed. He was not supposed to really be in love with Arja, after all, and while she enjoyed their banter, Bjorn knew there was nothing real behind it—not on her side, anyway.

"Well, you might have a point," she said. "I'll see if I can find more out."

"Tomorrow," Bjorn said, looking out to the dark horizon. "We need to sleep."

Arja sighed. "Assuming we'll be able to sleep at all, that is."

Hours had passed since she'd woken up, but Arja still listened to the rhythmic lull of the sea with a sense of wonder. Above her, the sailors continued to row. Their oars continually turned through the water in even, coordinated movements, and she might have welcomed the music of the water lapping had it not been for the nightmares that haunted her.

Every time she drifted off to sleep, it was only a matter of moments before the guilt gnawing in her gut roared in vengeful neglect, and she would see Sterlig's face—and then Jon's, and then Finnar's.

Arja gritted her teeth. Finnar had told her before that Sterlig had been unable to sleep during the three days it took to get to Eydis. She didn't want to know what kept him up, even though she doubted it had to do with inner shame or fear.

Sterlig had always been so sure of himself. Even in her dreams, when she saw him face death, he always appeared shocked more than afraid.

On the other side of the cargo hold, Finnar murmured quietly but painfully in his sleep.

Arja sighed. She was grateful she'd managed to keep herself quiet while the others slept. Earlier, she'd tended to Finnar as he muttered in his sleep, tucking her cloak around him so he would stop thrashing. The thick fur of her cloak buffered him against the side of the ship, even if it left her cold.

She glanced over at her would-be husband, amused and frustrated at the same time. Bjorn had leaned back against the other side of the cargo net beside her, careful to keep some distance from her. He slept more peacefully than her brothers, but there was no mistaking the beads of sweat on his forehead as his eyelids sporadically twitched in obvious discomfort.

"Bjorn?" Arja scooted over closer to him, debating whether she wanted to wake him up or not. But as she gazed at him, she decided not to disturb him. She brushed a lock of his hair back from his face, letting her fingers brush against his cheek, where a small patch of whiskers was slowly growing.

The people of Kyvan had considered Sterlig to be the more desirable sibling; he was stronger, with his larger frame. His brashness had been complemented by his looks. He'd had a strong face, with sharp lines and a straight nose, eyes that easily squinted in distaste or narrowed with challenge. He'd kept a beard, a short one slightly darker than his brownish hair with its golden highlights. His looks added to the considerably exaggerated tales of his exploits.

Keyvak had taught his son well, Arja thought with a grimace, recalling some of the last conversations she'd had with Sterlig.

She was a little surprised she had a hard time picturing him inside her mind. If there was anything Arja remembered clearly, it was how Sterlig's eyes were light brown. She recalled this clearly because some of the girls in town—including Gilda—had said his eyes glittered gold in the sunshine.

Arja huffed at the memory, struggling not to laugh. She told Gilda back then even if it was gold, she didn't want to dig through the muddy waste to get to it. Gilda had been speechless, horrified by Arja's comment, and Arja laughed even harder at her reaction.

Bjorn's eyes never made her think of mud or animal waste.

Arja bit back another laugh. *That's good, considering I'm pretending to be his wife. Wives should never look into their husbands' eyes and think of animal waste.*

She glanced back at Bjorn and carefully reached out to touch the ends of his wild hair, recalling the copper tints to his hair while he'd worked, remembering the gemlike quality of his eyes as he smiled at her. Bjorn liked to work, and his talent with smithing and metallurgy had eventually won him approval from Kyvan.

He had grown up largely looked over in favor of Sterlig, and Sterlig had cast a long shadow. But others were starting to take more notice of Bjorn this past season. He was a trader and a metalworker of note, and as he increasingly looked for work to pay off his father's drinking debts, the townspeople had embraced him and his unfortunate plight.

And his other features, too, Arja, thought, recalling how Gilda had practically offered herself and her bed to Bjorn.

She began to stroke Bjorn's hair lightly, not enough so he'd notice, secretly glad they'd left Kyvan before some other girl had found a way to enchant him.

Of course, Arja chastised herself, she'd more or less offered the same thing, except she'd suggested marriage. Finnar's earlier comments had stung, and Arja hated how right her brother was in his assessment.

It felt awful, thinking that Bjorn would equate her offer with the one from Gilda, where wedding her was the same as bedding her.

This is all Sterlig's fault. She glanced back over at Finn, who let out another terrified moan. Arja held her breath, wondering if he would wake up again, but a few moments passed, and Finnar stayed asleep.

Bjorn shuddered, and Arja quickly drew back her hand from his hair. She went still, but when she saw the small sliver of moonlight flicker against Bjorn's sleepy eyes, she knew he had stirred.

Arja watched him reach down to his belt and pull a small object from his coin pouch. Arja looked to see it was the small, golden crucifix his mother had given him.

Bjorn would reach for a cross before the sword, she thought, glancing down at his weapon, which lay on the floor next to him.

Arja gasped. It glowed with a flicker of green.

"Arja?" Bjorn shifted uncomfortably when he saw her sitting beside to him. "I didn't cry out, did I?"

"You were having some fits," Arja said, hurrying to explain why she was next to him. "I just came over to check on you. Sorry if I woke you."

Bjorn gave her a tired smile. "You almost never apologize, so I suppose I should give in and forgive you this time."

"Well, sorry for being concerned about you," Arja huffed. "You're not the only one who has issues sleeping, you know."

Bjorn took her arm before she could shuffle away from him. "I was just teasing. I didn't realize you were having nightmares, too. Come here."

He pulled her down next to him, letting her lean against his shoulder as he wrapped his arm around her. She fought against him, but only half-heartedly.

"You don't have to comfort me," Arja said, as his head fell lightly on hers.

"I'm the weak one between us, remember?" His voice was husky with weariness, but the sound of it stirred warmth inside her. "Perhaps I wanted you to comfort me."

"I suppose." Arja stole another peek at the sword. It no longer glowed. She relaxed a little, but she still resisted the urge to sleep.

"What's wrong?" he grunted.

"I'm not hurting you, am I?" Arja reached up and patted his arm. A rough red line stood up against the rest of his flesh near the top of his shoulder. "This is where … I hurt you, wasn't it?"

"It doesn't bother me. I took the bandage off earlier."

"Oh, Bjorn." Arja leaned over and carefully placed a soft kiss the wound. Bjorn's eyes went wide with her caress, and she hid a small smile from him.

A new thought struck her. "What if Finn wakes up?"

"He knows we're supposed to be married."

"I meant if he wake up from his nightmares."

"Then we'll wake up, too." Bjorn sighed into her hair. "Until then, sleep. We've got a lot to do in the next two days. You'll need your rest. I know I do."

Arja laughed quietly. "I guess it is strange to think it was only yesterday I came to see you in your forge."

"Strange doesn't begin to describe it." Bjorn pressed a sleepy, smiling kiss to her forehead. *"Kona."*

At his playful endearment, Arja swallowed hard. Guilt suddenly suffocated her, hard and fast, as she thought about how she did not deserve Bjorn's kindness. His flirtatious teasing, while it was meant in jest, stung more than a blow.

Her heart clenched as he leaned against her.

Maybe ... it would be better, if I told him the truth.

She bit her lip, too scared to say anything; the thought alone was frightening.

But being afraid was not something she believed in. Living in fear was not living at all—and that was why she had been compelled to take off on this journey. She would not fear the dragon, even if it took Sterlig's life.

But there was something she feared, more than her own life. And as terrifying as it was to contemplate, she had to face her fear.

"Bjorn?" Arja whispered, straightening up.

No answer. He was asleep again.

Arja sighed. She would have to tell him, she thought. But not right now.

Not when he's like this.

Arja stared at him, taking in his full profile, before she gradually drifted off to sleep, too.

For the first time in weeks, she did not have any nightmares.

THE LEGEND OF EYDIS

<u>10</u>

✿   ✿   ✿

"So, you want to know more about the legend of Eydis?"

"Yes, if you can tell me." Bjorn stood behind Camille, helping him hoist the main sail. The storm from the day before had washed over, but there was still plenty of wind, which excited Camille. He'd told Bjorn earlier they'd be able to make up for lost time from the day before.

But after Camille tied off the sail, he groaned, nodding upward. "There's another tear up near the top."

"I see it. Let me get it," Arja offered, stepping up behind them. She gave Bjorn a quick glare, warning him not to object.

Despite her fuss, Bjorn felt content. He'd managed to get her to listen yesterday, when the storm endangered everyone. With the calmer weather, he did not mind if she worked on the deck. And fixing the sail was a good task for her; Arja was a strong climber, and her years of sewing and working with her mother helped.

"Go ahead and tell us what you know about the legend of Eydis," Arja said, grabbing Camille's dagger from its sheath at his side. Before he could object, she held up a roll of extra rope and began climbing up the mast. "I'll listen from above."

"Arja and I have heard the legend all our lives, but we would love to hear you tell it," Bjorn added.

Ephraim sniffed loudly from behind him. "Camille does like to hear the sound of his own voice."

"Well, what other music can compare?" Camille said with a laugh, even though there was an uneasy look in his dark eyes and a flushed look to his dark-skinned cheeks. "I will ask for something in return."

Bjorn hesitated. "If it's money—"

"No." Camille looked up at Arja. "I'd like something from you, my friend. A story for a story, if you will."

Arja looped the twine through the sail, still effortlessly perched on the mast. "What kind of story?"

"You'll see." Camille gave her a smug look. "If I'm going to tell you what you want, I get to decide. Perhaps a humiliating memory?"

"Finnar would love that." Arja scowled at him, before she glanced at Bjorn, who gave her a resigned shrug. "All right, but you go first," she snapped, before she went back to the task at hand.

Bjorn let out a small sigh of relief. He was glad she was cooperating.

"As you know, a hundred years ago, Eydis was part of the larger island of Snæland, and it was ruled

THE LEGEND OF EYDIS

over by a wealthy king from the Norselands, and his daughter, Princess Brynja, was the most beautiful woman in all the world."

"Of course she's beautiful and rich," Arja said.

"Arja." Bjorn laughed. "You are, too."

"Ouch." Arja's hand slipped at his compliment, and then she glared down at him. "Don't distract Camille, Bjorn. Let him tell the story."

Camille and Bjorn exchanged an amused look, and then Camille continued.

"The princess's aging father agreed to her marriage with Prince Andor of Oseberg."

"I told you it wouldn't take much to get him started," Ephraim muttered, before leaving with another huff. "I'll be at the stern, preparing for the next storm. Hopefully his foolishness won't get us killed this time."

"You know we will be fine," Camille snapped after him.

Ephraim waved back at him dismissively, but Camille ignored him, turning back to Bjorn and Arja.

"Forgive me. As I was saying, Princess Brynja was the most beautiful woman in the world, and many suitors sought her hand in marriage. Prince Andor knew what a treasure he'd been given."

Bjorn listened as he watched Arja, who was still working on repairing the broken sail.

"The princess was grateful for the match, too," Camille continued. "For she was in love with the young prince. They married, and all seemed well—until the prince was killed by bandits in the kingdom.

"Over a hundred years had passed since Eydis had been broken off from the mainland. Without a ruler, the warriors had quickly fought each other for power, and it was only in the last two generations the Thordirsson family brought order and became the island's chieftain."

"Who was it, Camille, that fought the prince?" Bjorn asked. "I've never heard who it was; I mean, I don't recall any names."

"If I told you, you would not believe me," Camille said. "I know many of them, and they are all simple townsfolk."

"Townsfolk?" Bjorn frowned. More than once, he'd seen the rage of ordinary people in the face of injustice or temptation, and he knew the soul's fury was not unique to warriors. "What do you mean you know them?"

Camille shook his head. "Perhaps you'll see what I mean later, my friend. The people rebelled, and Prince Andor was killed. His spirit left his body and took flight in the form of an eagle, before it made its way to Brynja's palace, where she wept. At her anger, his spirit transformed, and the dragon appeared."

"But it's a female dragon," Bjorn said. "You said that before."

Camille nodded. "And that—"

He stopped talking, and his eyes began to bulge. Bjorn saw him swallow hard; he clenched his arm, covering his tattoo.

"Camille?" Arja jumped down between them.

"Something's wrong," Bjorn whispered, but Camille only held out his hand to Bjorn.

"Your sword," he gasped.

Confused, Bjorn pulled the sword out and handed it to Camille, who took it and then thrust it into the heart of his tattoo.

"Camille!" Arja cried out in horror, and Bjorn moved to shield her from the sight. She twisted around him, but kept her hand on his arm as she watched Camille press the tip of Bjorn's sword further into his skin.

"That's enough," Ephraim shouted. "Get him down in the hold. Now."

"No," Camille hissed. "It's fine. It's working, Ephraim. This sword has tasted the true blood of the dragon. I can feel her anger."

Bjorn felt his mouth drop open. The sword glowed green, while Camille's skin began to burn with a crimson aura.

"You're just going to kill yourself, and the rest of us, too," Ephraim yelled.

"Let me help," Arja offered, but Camille shook his head.

"I don't need it," he gasped out, heaving as he struggled to catch his breath. "Look."

"No!" Ephraim objected, as Camille pulled the dagger out of his arm.

Bjorn tugged Arja back, worried Camille's blood would spill on her. But he saw a second later, there was no need to worry.

Camille's skin was split deeply, but no blood flowed.

"What?" Bjorn took hold of his arm, carefully looking it over. No matter how he moved it, there was no blood.

"It still hurts, even if it's not bleeding," Camille muttered, taking his hand back.

"Sorry." Bjorn apologized, still staring at Camille's wound.

"This is the end," Ephraim murmured. "Oh, no, no, no, no, no! This is the end!"

"Stop, Ephraim." Camille sighed. "This has to be done."

"We're all going to die!"

"We are already dead!"

Camille's words hung in the air, echoing with stinging silence.

"What are you talking about?" Bjorn finally asked.

Despite Ephraim's enraged look, Camille answered him. "The dragon has taken our blood for her own use."

"Stop saying these things. Please, I beg you, Camille." Ephraim fell to the floor beside him. "She will kill us if you say too much."

"I know when to stop, Ephraim."

"Clearly, you don't. I want to live, Camille."

"We haven't lived in years. Not since we pledged our loyalty to Eydis and the princess." Camille turned to Bjorn. "I saw you carry a crucifix from Oseberg."

Bjorn put his hand over the pouch on his belt, where he carried his mother's gift. "Yes. My mother gave it to me."

"Andor was from Oseberg," Camille said. "The one with honorable heart is the only one who can slay the dragon. Seeing as you've married Arja here, and you are dedicated to her, I believe you will be able to overcome the dragon of Eydis."

Bjorn and Arja exchanged a worried glance, and he felt more unprepared than ever before.

How many times, Bjorn wondered, had Arja called him weak, or Sterlig had triumphed over him in their sparring battles? He could read and he knew how to work metal, but he was far from the best Viking or warrior available. And while Camille had called him honorable and said he was determined to protect Arja—which he was, as he owed that to her as Sterlig's former intended wife—he was also lying about being married to her.

"Yes. I do believe you will succeed." Camille nodded. "As that is the case, I will do what I can to help—even if it means I will die."

He grimaced in pain again, and Bjorn saw the tattoo on his arm turn blood red, while Camille's face blanched.

"That's enough for now." Ephraim stepped between Camille and the others. "Camille can't say anything further about this. Leave him. We have a ship to run, and don't think I wouldn't toss you overboard if I could."

"Camille would not forgive you," Arja said.

Ephraim drew himself up to his full height, only to look down his nose at her. "You know nothing about us, lady. And you know less than nothing about Eydis."

He turned on his heel and walked away.

Once he was gone, Camille fell down on the deck and laughed—a dry, humorless chortle, instead of his usual, full-bellied laugh. "Not all disasters are the same, are they? Your cross is proof of such a thing."

"Are you better?" Bjorn asked, kneeling down next to him.

"Now that Ephraim's left me alone? Absolutely." Camille gave him a small smile. "The man has been my best friend for decades and I'm still not entirely sure why."

"Not sure why he's your friend, or why someone else hasn't killed him?" Arja asked. As Camille laughed, she took hold of his arm. "Let me see your wound."

"It's healed, but I will need to rest before I work," Camille told her. "No need to trouble me about my arm, but I do believe you owe me. I'd think it's only fair to ask for my story now, especially after you've seen the price of such knowledge."

Arja pursed her lips, clearly hesitating.

"I can tell you a story," Bjorn offered, but Camille frowned.

"That was not our agreed terms," Camille said. "It's your turn to uphold your honor, Arja. So tell me how you fell in love with Bjorn."

Bjorn felt his heart seize up in unexpected pressure. What would Arja say? He fully expected her to ignore the request, or insist that it was too personal, but when she nodded, he found himself waiting for her answer, too.

"All right." Arja kept her eyes focused on Camille as she agreed to his request. "I'll tell you."

Bjorn watched as she patted Camille's arm, the one he had sliced open. It was healed now, with only the barest pink lines of a scar marking the place where he'd plunged his sword. As he watched, Arja carefully twisted Camille's arm, turning the tattooed side of his arm away from sight.

"Perhaps you should go check on Finn, Bjorn." She put on her sweetest, deadliest smile as she looked back at him. "Yes, why don't you do that? I'll see to Camille."

"No." Camille motioned for Bjorn to stay put. "He should stay, in case you intend to kill me."

Arja arched her brow. "But I thought you can't die? Or that you were already dead?"

"Still, wouldn't that be more temptation for you? I am not immune to pain, just death."

"Perhaps you have a point," Arja muttered, making Bjorn smile.

As much as he knew Arja was more compassionate than she let on, Bjorn was also familiar with her temper, and he smiled, imagining how much she would lash out at Camille if she could.

"See?" Camille laughed. "Just let him stay."

Bjorn's smile disappeared. Arja would have to lie about how she was in love with him, and he didn't know if he really wanted to hear it, especially if she used Sterlig for inspiration. It would hurt him, but he worried it would hurt Arja more.

But then, Arja had lost Sterlig, just as Princess Brynja had lost Andor. Perhaps sharing their grief would allow them some comfort. He knew her well, and a woman with her temperament might have more in common with the dragon guarding Eydis than the princess under its protection.

"So, tell me your story." Camille nudged her. "I'm sure it's a good one."

As unpleasant as he feared Arja's tale would be, Bjorn was curious, and subconsciously leaned forward as she began her story.

THE LEGEND OF EYDIS

11

◎　　　◎　　　◎

Arja hated how she could feel Bjorn watching her. There was nothing she wanted more in that moment than to make him leave; there was no comfort in knowing she could always explain herself later, reminding him that this was part of their charade and she didn't have to mean any of what she said.

She also didn't like being this close to Camille's tattoo. It was further proof Bjorn had been right before—they needed a better plan for when they landed on Eydis. It was also proof that she owed Camille something, and he enjoyed having her in his debt.

And what a debt it was, too. His life was at risk, but he was still willing to help them. She hated it, but she knew when she was trapped.

So Arja began to talk of Bjorn—how they'd grown up as neighbors and eventually became friends thanks to their brothers, and how she wanted to learn from them, and all while Camille listened, patiently fascinated.

"So, when did you begin to fall in love?" Camille asked. "Growing up together is one thing. Growing in love is another."

Arja batted her eyes at Bjorn playfully. "How could I resist?"

"No, no." Camille shook his head. "Tell me the details."

"Well … " Arja took a deep breath. She had accepted this, but she had to make it convincing for Camille's sake. "I suppose it started the winter after my thirteenth summer. My father had sailed to the northern coast of Snæland with Sterlig and Bjorn's father, and my brothers were in charge of protecting the house. But my mother was carrying Gunnar, one of my younger brothers, and she went into labor."

"I remember that night, too." Bjorn looked thoughtful. "Finn came to my house just as my uncle arrived for a visit. That was the year he started training me in the forge."

"Yes, that's right. So Bjorn and his mother and his uncle all came over to help my mother," Arja agreed. "We'd thought she had another month before the baby would come, but she began bleeding and her water broke."

Arja clenched her fists tightly as she remembered Elska's white face when Geira began to worry she would have a stillborn babe. Elska had lost several of her own babies before, and Arja didn't want to see both women suffer.

Bjorn came up beside her. "My mother discovered it was a breech baby."

"I'm telling the story, remember?" Arja struggled not to snap at him too harshly, but she was already trembling. "The following hours were some of the worst of my mother's life, and certainly my own, too."

Bjorn took her hand and carefully uncurled her fist. He held onto her hand and Arja swallowed hard; she couldn't say if he was making her task more easy or more difficult.

With more composure than she would've thought possible, Arja recounted how Geira screamed and Bjorn's mother helped with the birth. Lodd had prepared a dagger in heat, so they were ready if they needed to cut her open to save the baby.

"What I remember most is Bjorn holding onto me as we waited for some kind of resolution, never knowing if it would be a happy one or not," Arja said, tightening her hold on Bjorn's as she looked away from Camille.

For hours, long into the night, they stayed outside the Gilsson longhouse, terrified and unable to move away while Geira finally gave birth to Gunnar.

"Bjorn had been there for me, and I was grateful for his support." Arja gave Bjorn a tender smile. Even then, she'd known he would protect her. "It meant a lot to me."

"I see," Camille said, making Arja flinch.

"That's when I told Bjorn I never want to have children," Arja said. "Gunnar ended up being just like my other brothers, giving us poop and tears for months on end. And after carrying them for nearly a year? No, I'd rather be a shieldmaiden and risk everything on the battleground."

She looked at Bjorn now, silently daring him to interrupt her, but he only gave her an encouraging nod.

"And when I said that, Bjorn agreed with me," Arja said. "He's the only one who's ever let me be who I wanted to be. No one ever took me seriously about that."

"But surely you'd change your mind?" Camille chuckled, irritating Arja with his flippancy.

"Everyone's always said that," Arja huffed. "*Everyone*. My mother, father, brothers. Even Sterlig said that."

"Have you?" Camille asked. "Especially now that you are married?"

For the first time, Arja hesitated. She knew she had to tell a convincing story,

That was when Bjorn spoke up. "We are hoping to go on more adventures before we think about having children. But either way, I am more than happy to have her."

Arja's mouth dropped open, and she gaped at Bjorn. When he gave her a small smirk, she snapped out of her shock.

"And that's it," she concluded. "That's the story."

"What a lovely one, too," Camille said. "And I thank you for telling me. But, I must ask, why are you so determined to get to Eydis, if you are happy in your love?"

"That's another story." Arja blushed furiously. "And if you'll excuse me, I'd like to go check on Finn now. It's been a few hours since I've seen him."

"Wait. By now you should know, the power that binds me and my life," Camille said softly. He took hold of Arja's hand and placed it in Bjorn's, holding them together as he stood there. "You've seen it."

Once more, Arja remembered the greenish glint to Bjorn's blade.

She glanced down at Camille's arm again, watching as it sparkled with a reddish tint.

"When we get to Eydis, you will need to find Pyri." Beads of sweat formed on Camille's forehead, and his breathing started to sound constricted.

"Camille," Arja said, suddenly alarmed. She looked around for help, but none of the other sailors paid them any mind. "What's wrong?"

"Stop talking to us." Bjorn grabbed Camille by the shoulders. "It's not worth your life."

Camille's dark eyes closed. "I've already told you, my life is gone. But the least I can do is send you to Pyri. Tell her I sent you, and she'll be able to help."

"Pyri?" Arja repeated the name carefully, as Camille nodded.

Another grimace appeared on his face as his dragon tattoo raged with angry light. He jerked away from them, gasping hard as he propelled himself toward the bow. "This is the last thing I ask of you, and the last thing I can give you. Please, honor my request."

"We will," Bjorn promised. His hand tightened around hers, and Arja flinched.

Between Camille's sacrifice and Bjorn's determination, she wanted to weep and rage at her own shame and fear.

It's all too much.

Camille was cursed by the dragon and doomed to feed it through his own blood until the dragon was killed, and she had to face the wave of emotions she'd unearthed from telling him about Bjorn.

The story she'd given Camille was the truth, and the vividness of the memory left her vulnerable, especially at the way Bjorn had assured Camille they were not thinking of children. She knew it was not real, but Arja could have kissed him when he stood up for her like that. Some men felt it was justified to punish their wives or take lovers if their wives did not have children. It pained her to think of Bjorn's own father, and how Elska had been treated after her stillborn births and miscarriages. Bjorn had turned out so different from his father— and his brother, too.

"Arja?" Bjorn stood in front of her.

Arja felt her heart stir with longing as she stared at him. The desire to kiss him, to hold onto him, hit her hard, leaving her breathless and mystified.

Bjorn put his hand on her arm. "Are you all right?"

"This is getting complicated." She shook her head. Arja didn't like feeling vulnerable.

Vulnerability led to foolish decisions, and she had been reckless enough already.

"I hope that wasn't too hard for you."

"What? Oh, you mean the story?" Arja shrugged, hating herself as she realized her hands were still shaking. "Don't worry about it, Bjorn. I'm not without my wits."

"I know that. I meant … I didn't want you to lie, because of Sterlig. That's all."

He said it with such an annoying amount of care and concern that Arja felt her temper flare. She didn't want his pity.

Not now. Not after the story she'd told.

"I'm fine." Her voice was so calm and stoic she wondered if she had to hear herself say it to believe it. "I know Camille thinks I'm a liar and a cheat, but I didn't have to lie about that memory."

"What are you—"

But at the last second, something broke inside of her. The thought of losing his warmth and kindness devastated her, and Arja couldn't bear it. She stopped pulling away and rebounded, plunging herself back into his arms. He was already embracing her when she lifted her face and pressed her lips to his.

She'd meant to shock him, but she ended up surprised, too, as Bjorn responded to her. Without hesitation, he leaned into her kiss, his mouth moving over hers provocatively and possessively. His hands moved up and down her back, tangled in her hair, cradled her face. It was the kiss of a true lover, and it was such a contrast to his usual demeanor that she lost herself, intoxicated by his scent, his taste, his touch—and her own overwhelming desire.

He was always so much bigger than he seemed; Arja held onto him tightly, letting her hands dig into his back, her fingers pressing into his tunic, feeling the hard muscles of his back. His arms wound around her, enveloping her in a place of refuge, a cocoon of fire and warmth that felt too hot to be safe, but too irresistible to step away.

"Arja, I—"

She silenced Bjorn with another kiss. She didn't want him to say anything; she was weak enough. If he did anything more to break the armor around her heart, she would shatter completely.

Bjorn was kissing her as though he loved her.

It had to be enough.

She didn't deserve anything else. Not from Bjorn.

He wouldn't kiss me like this if he knew the truth.

At that thought, breathless and ashamed, Arja pulled herself free.

"I need to check on Finn," she said, hurrying off before he could stop her.

As she headed down the stairs into the cargo hold, the other sailors watched her, and she hated how helpless she felt.

There were perils ahead of them, just waiting on Eydis, and Arja would have to be extra careful once they arrived. She'd already been careless enough with her heart; she couldn't lose her head, too.

12

⸭   ⸭   ⸭

That night, Bjorn's dreams were eager to welcome him.

He saw Sterlig's face as he fell to the ground again. Visceral fear filled his brother's eyes, and stress carved lines on his face. Bjorn watched as Sterlig grasped the bloody sword in his hand, and then he submitted to death and sorrow.

Bjorn jolted awake. He rubbed his eyes clear and wiped the sweat off his brow. He was surprised to find Arja next to him, still sleeping. Her head leaned against his shoulder, and he quickly forced himself to remain still; he didn't want to wake her, especially over his nightmares.

Her blonde hair, pale in the dim light of the hold, fell across her eyes, the loosened tresses twitching as she breathed in and out. After their earlier kiss, she had done her best to avoid him; he hadn't been surprised when he'd come down for bed and saw she was already asleep.

He grinned as he thought about their kiss, remembering his surprise when she reached for him, and her own surprise when he began kissing her back.

He had not been expecting that level of sincerity from her story, and Bjorn was encouraged that Arja had not once mentioned she'd fallen in love with Sterlig, or how his brother had vowed to go to Eydis and slay the dragon for her.

Her silence gave him hope she might find peace about Sterlig's death, and Bjorn took her kiss as proof she might truly fall in love with him one day.

He watched her now, as the *Sea Serpent* pushed along the sea waters. There was only a little light coming into the hold, and the little there was lingered around his sword unnaturally.

Bjorn took hold of the eagle-shaped pommel. He saw the greenish glow encircle his hand and then fade into the air.

Arja shifted against him, and she let out a soft sigh.

Bjorn let go of his sword before placing a helpless kiss on her forehead.

"I'll never understand why you like her, you know." Finnar's voice was quiet, but it echoed from across the hold. "She'll run you into the ground with her nagging."

Bjorn shrugged. "Some materials need to be hammered, if you're going to make them useful."

"Arja's a good hammer, but I doubt she's enough of a knowledgeable blacksmith when it comes to you. She might enjoy that power too much." Finnar laughed quietly. "Besides, you're plenty useful as it is, Bjorn. Not like me. I'm just stuck here."

"You can only do so much right now if you're going to stay alive. Besides, your value isn't determined by your usefulness." Bjorn looked back down at Arja, tenderly watching her for signs of waking. "There are plenty of things more important than usefulness. Like honor."

"You're a good man, Bjorn. Since the gods seem content to play with us as they will, it is good for you to be concerned with honor. I can't honestly say what they enjoy more, watching a man's spirit break or seeing one that is able to stand up against them."

"My mother taught me differently."

"Oh, yes." Finnar let out a weary sigh. "I'd forgotten about that. But what is the real difference between the Christian god and the gods of Odin and our people's history? We are still facing down a dragon and a curse."

"If there's any difference, it's that I know dragons can be defeated, curses can be broken, and even death can be defeated," Bjorn said. He reached down and pulled out the small crucifix from his pouch. The gold winked at him, and he thought of his mother. "There are demons in this world who would have us believe we are at their mercy, but in truth, they themselves are at the mercy of God. As are we. But God is loving towards us, like a father to his children. The others thrive on our fear."

"But we are still at the mercy of a supernatural power, no matter what you believe." Finnar stood up and walked closer to Bjorn. "And perhaps he's the same kind of father as yours?"

"The Christian God and those of Valhalla are still not the same." Bjorn shuffled the golden cross back into his pouch carefully.

"Yes, one asks for your life, and the others ask for your death." Finnar glanced away, looking toward the stairs. "Right now, I am not sure which is better."

Bjorn frowned. Finnar was usually so quick to laugh or make others laugh; it was not like him to wallow in his despair. Bjorn thought of the desperation he'd seen in his friend's eyes back at Kyvan. So far, Finnar was safe, nestled inside the *Sea Serpent*, and if there was a demonic power calling him to his death, Finnar had managed to avoid it so far.

"I feel awful, you know," Finnar admitted quietly, with a resigned sadness in his voice. "And not just because I dare not seek the sun or sea while I am on this boat."

"What do you mean?"

"Sterlig was one of my best friends. I feel some responsibility for his death, too."

"Sterlig would be the first to say you're robbing him of his rightful glory," Bjorn said carefully. He looked back down at his sword, thinking of his dream again. He wanted to give Finnar a reason to remain hopeful, even if their situation looked bleak. "Even though my brother is dead, he still would want the honor of dying for love and facing down a great beast."

"If you ask me, he lost his honor the moment we arrived on Eydis." Finnar let out a dismissive snort. "He didn't have a plan, and he was restless the entire time we were in the knarr, too. And when he saw Brynja the Bride, he forgot about Arja entirely."

"What?" Bjorn leaned closer, uncertain he'd heard Finnar correctly. "What did you say?"

"Sterlig started chasing after the princess the moment he landed on Eydis," Finnar said. "I guess it wasn't all right away, but he couldn't stop thinking of her after he saw her."

Camille's earlier warning made more sense now. The old sailor was hopeful, since he believed that Bjorn had married Arja and devoted himself to her happiness. No doubt Camille thought he was dimwitted to follow Arja's lead, but that supposed deficiency could also play out as a boon, if he slayed the dragon and set Camille and the others free.

"I've never heard you talk about what happened on Eydis like this before." Bjorn struggled to keep his voice even; he wanted Finnar to explain, but he was also stunned by his admission.

"I didn't want Arja to know. I didn't know she even wanted to marry him until Sterlig told me." Finnar nodded over at his sister, still leaning on Bjorn's shoulder. "She's good at hiding things if you let her."

"So are you, apparently."

"True." Finnar rubbed his chin. "Probably a family trait. But we have good intentions."

"That's why you never told her about Sterlig and the princess. You didn't want to hurt Arja."

"Yes."

Bjorn slumped forward, ever so slightly. As much as he loved his friend, Bjorn couldn't help but feel betrayed by his silence. He'd believed Sterlig had died honorably, remaining loyal to Arja up to the end of his life. If he had known the truth, he might have acted differently.

Finnar pointed at Bjorn's sword. "I figured your heart was a little tougher than hers would be, even if it was broken. That's what your sword's inscription says, right? 'Broken heart.'"

Bjorn's jaw clenched. He'd been sharpening the blade, finishing up the final touches of his own weapon when Sterlig had burst into his forge and formally announced his upcoming marriage to Arja.

Hearing he'd lost her to Sterlig—like so many other things—he'd stayed behind in his forge another half-day, adding the inscription in the old runic letters.

Broken heart.

"Sterlig thought it was a blessing for health," Finnar said with a snort.

"I told him to learn to read properly," Bjorn murmured softly. "I guess he knew some. My mother found some scrolls about the legend of Eydis with his belongings after you and Jon returned."

"Well, maybe he did have a better plan than just go and kill the dragon, then," Finnar replied. "Of course, if he did, he failed to follow that plan even more than the plan to stay true to my sister. He got me and Jon to buy some perfume for her, and then he gave it to the princess."

Arja sighed softly and Bjorn held his breath, hoping she hadn't woken up. He could understand Finnar's decision to remain quiet about Sterlig's actions; Bjorn didn't want her to be hurt, either.

When he was fairly certain Arja was still asleep, he turned his attention back to Finnar.

"What else happened?"

Finnar shook his head. "It was too late. The princess tossed his sword out of her castle, and it fell to the ground. Then this little girl came up to us and gave us the sword. She then told us to take it back to his family so they would know the truth of what happened. She was such a weird little girl, too. She had dark hair and these wide eyes, but she seemed too young to be handing out swords."

Bjorn frowned and put his hand on his sword, anger stirring as he thought about his brother's betrayal. He thought back to his dream again, never having noticed much besides Sterlig's last breaths, and the sword lying on the ground.

But at Finnar's description, something tugged in his mind.

Before they'd left for Eydis, before Arja even approached him with her offer of marriage, he'd been dreaming of Sterlig's battle. He saw the dragon, he saw Sterlig's fall—and at the side of the battlefield, there was something else. There was a little flicker of white, and as he thought about it, he saw a little girl in a white dress. She watched Sterlig die, wearing a smirk so devious he recoiled at the thought.

Was she the little girl Finnar was talking about?

And if she was, why did she seem so happy as his brother died?

But then, hearing how he'd forgotten Arja, perhaps he could understand how someone could take pleasure in his death.

A moment later, Bjorn shook his head. It was not good of him to give into that temptation, he told himself.

"All I ask of you, Bjorn, if you truly love my sister, is that you will tell her and keep her safe." Finnar gave him a smirk. "But then, you've already done that, and I know I can trust you to keep your word, can't I? You are an honorable man."

Before Bjorn could reply, Finnar groaned and leaned forward as he rubbed his back. "I hope Jon is doing well. I envy him, really. Even if he's still recovering, he gets to lay down in proper bedding."

"I'm sure he will be well. Your family is not like mine." Bjorn cleared his throat. "I mean, at least your father is a good man."

"That's true. I mean, I'm not there, but I'm sure they'll make him stay home until they hear about us," Finnar said. "I'm not sure what they'll do if I die, though. I can see my father and brothers trying to come and avenge us."

"I think it's safe to say my father won't come to avenge me," Bjorn said glumly.

"Yes." Finnar snorted. "He didn't even try for Sterlig, did he?"

Bjorn said nothing. Finnar was right, and there was nothing Bjorn could do about that any longer. His father had rejected him, and Bjorn couldn't help but think perhaps it was one of God's mercies.

I will never be the kind of father to my children the way my father was to me.

If he ever had children, that was. Bjorn looked over at Arja and vowed he would never be the kind of husband his father was to his mother, either.

"Hey down there! You should get up."
Camille's voice rang throughout the hold, and Bjorn
welcomed the announcement. "Eydis is in sight."

"I don't know if I really want to see it again."
Finnar shuddered. "But I will be glad to get out of
this boat again."

"That seems to be a good sign," Bjorn agreed.
He nudged Arja carefully. "Arja."

Her eyelids fluttered open, and Bjorn's heart
began to beat faster.

"What is it, Bjorn?" Her voice was quiet and sad
as she looked up at him, and he wished he could
kiss her until she smiled again.

Instead, he cleared his throat. "We're here."

❖   ❖   ❖

The rumors of Eydis and its beauty were
nothing compared to its reality. The morning light
broke over the horizon, outlining the small castle
tower with light. Arja stood with Bjorn at the peak
of the *Sea Serpent's* prow in reverent, stunned
silence.

Arja studied the castle, where Princess Brynja
lived. She was rarely, if ever, outside her tower.
Arja studied the small balcony at the top, wondering
if the princess would reveal herself to them. It was
still early morning, and surely even princesses had
to sleep.

The tower looked strong, while the stone seemed old and worn. Vines dotted with small little flowers adorned the base, and the rest of the castle seemed to disappear into the mountain behind it.

"Look," Bjorn said. "There's the port."

At his prompting, Arja looked over at the small buildings and other boats tied down in a small cove. The boats there were all much smaller than the *Sea Serpent*.

"Beautiful, isn't it?" Camille asked, coming up behind them. "You'd never know such a fearsome beast resides under the island."

"Are you sure that's where she is?" Bjorn asked.

While Bjorn and Camille continued to talk, Arja kept her eyes on the shoreline. Although it was a sight that defied imagination, Arja found herself strangely glum as the island of Eydis came closer.

It was supposed to be a straightforward mission.

She was supposed to go to Eydis and confront the dragon who'd killed Sterlig. If she died, she didn't mind. It was better than staying at home and being stuck as a nursemaid to all of her brothers while only getting to train with Vidur's other shieldmaidens from time to time. Sleeping in a rocking ship and facing down a storm—not to mention coming face to face with the supernatural—had not deterred her in the least.

But as she looked over at Bjorn, guilt and uncertainty crept up to paralyze her.

Earlier, she'd woken up as Bjorn talked with Finnar. She found herself laying down next to Bjorn, and she didn't want to move away from him. He was warm, but he was also hers in that moment; so she listened to them talk about Sterlig and how he began to chase after the princess.

At first, she'd been merely irritated at Sterlig's attraction for the princess. She could understand, knowing him as she did, that he would fall for a beautiful, rich princess, especially if there was magic involved. But the more she thought about it, the more she hated him for it.

Bjorn would *never* do that to her. Or at least, she didn't think so. Not if he really loved her.

It certainly felt *right*—even though it wasn't the truth. But it was right enough that Arja felt alive, truly alive, for the first time in months, and now she wanted to live.

She wanted to live, and she wanted to be with Bjorn.

The honest admission cut through the lies she'd collected over the past several months, and the thought of facing down Eydis' dragon was more welcoming than admitting she would have to tell Bjorn the truth.

He would never really love her if he didn't know the truth, and if he knew the truth, he wouldn't love her at all—just like she didn't love Sterlig.

"Are you well, Arja?" Bjorn asked.

"Yes," she whispered, before clearing her throat. "Just … impressed. The island looks absolutely divine."

Ephraim let out a snort behind her. "Demonic, you mean."

Arja flinched, but Bjorn put his arm around her waist protectively.

"If the devil, Lucifer himself, was able to appear as an angel of light, then it makes sense that an island full of evil is hidden behind a mask of beauty."

Ephraim gave another indignant huff and turned away. It seemed for all Bjorn agreed with him, Ephraim remained determined to be disagreeable.

"Ignore him," Bjorn said. "Don't let him make you upset."

"I wasn't upset," Arja snapped. "Not about him, anyway."

"Still, you should calm down." He pulled her closer to him, and when she resisted, he added, "The others are watching, my beloved wife."

She narrowed her eyes before she gave up and relaxed against him. Her heart fluttered at his embrace. If they were really married, she would have been tempted to reach up and kiss him, and a

THE LEGEND OF EYDIS

pang of regret mixed bitterly with her delight at being so close to Bjorn.

"Once we land, we'll have to find Pyri," Bjorn said. "I'll ask around and say I need my sword sharpened. Surely if enough princes and soldiers come to try to conquer this place, there's a forge or an armory around."

"What should I do? Perhaps I can look for work." Arja looked around. She doubted there was any need for a shieldmaiden on an island that was protected by a dragon. She shuddered at the thought of working as a maid or a nurse. After all the years of helping her mother with her many brothers, she'd rather face the dragon.

Bjorn shook his head. "I want you to stay with Finnar and see if he remembers anything about Eydis from before. You'll be able to protect each other while I look for Pyri."

"I'd rather find work."

"Finnar *is* work." Bjorn gestured toward the gangplank, where her brother stood in a line of other sailors. His eyes were still red, but not glowing, and Arja watched him set foot on the deck without issue. Her brother even turned back and waved to her.

"Camille said we could stay with the ship," Arja reminded him. "Why not just stay here? We can find more information about slaying the dragon and then come back here."

"They have their own homes and routines to attend to," Bjorn said. "And we haven't decided whether or not we should slay the dragon at all."

"That's a lie. Of course we're going to kill the dragon." Arja scowled. "Why else did we come here?"

"We came here for you to find peace over Sterlig's death. That's not the same thing."

"What about the sailors of the *Sea Serpent*? They are bound to the dragon of Eydis, and we should set them free. I don't need peace, Bjorn. But they should be free."

"That was their choice, Arja." Bjorn's jaw clenched. "Choices have consequences, and we might not be able to help them."

"We should still try."

Bjorn sighed, but he nodded. "We'll try. In the meantime, we're working together on this, remember?"

Arja glanced back at the island, only to see a small flash of bright, white light at the top the castle tower.

Brynja the Bride.

She thought of how Finnar had said Sterlig was drawn to the princess, and as much as she was certain Bjorn could never love her, she wouldn't lose him to Brynja.

Arja pressed herself into Bjorn's chest, and wrapped her arm around his neck. "Of course I remember. I'm your wife. You wouldn't forget that, either, would you, *elskin mín?*"

She grinned as a slight blush appeared on Bjorn's cheeks. Arja was about to tease him again when he leaned down and kissed her firmly, and she forgot everything else.

His kiss didn't just feel right; it felt *real*, and she would've given anything in the world to make it true.

"Arja." Bjorn's voice was rough and soft as the magic between them came to an end, and Arja opened her eyes. "We'd better go."

She nodded and reluctantly stepped out of his embrace, forcing herself to focus on the task at hand.

She had come to slay the dragon of Eydis, to free her brothers—and herself—from its cursed memory, and to put Sterlig's memory to rest. It was a matter of honor on her part, to serve her family and rectify what Sterlig had ruined. And now, she thought, looking back to the *Sea Serpent*, it was also a matter of thanking her new friends by setting them free from the dragon's power.

"Arja?"

As determined as she was, her heart fluttered as Bjorn called to her. "What is it?"

"Make sure you go with Finn," Bjorn said. "From the look on his face, I might need you to protect me from him, too."

Arja glanced down. Her brother glared up at them, clearly upset. Though she assured Bjorn she would protect him from Finnar's anger, Arja had a feeling, as she stepped onto the gangplank, that Finnar's anger was likely for her, not Bjorn.

182

13

⚬   ⚬   ⚬

Bjorn disembarked from the *Sea Serpent* with a feeling of unease. Eydis was as mysterious and enchanting as he'd heard, and it seemed strange that his brother's death did nothing to deter his appreciation for the island itself.

He watched Finnar and Arja head off together, both of them armed with swords and shields. He did not like leaving Arja, even if she was with her brother; their journey here already proof she was capable of escaping Finnar's watch.

But as Arja's blonde hair caught the sunshine of the day, and she laughed loudly at one of Finnar's remarks—probably something about her safety— Bjorn felt the pull in his gut.

He was in love with her, as he had always been, and he could not lose her. Not again.

Bjorn looked down at his sword, which he carried at his side. When Sterlig had come racing into his forge, bragging about how Arja had agreed to marry him, Bjorn had felt the world fall away from under his feet. He had managed to stay calm, offer his congratulations to Sterlig, and then move through the motions of his life—even as Keyvak fought with Sterlig over his choice of bride, Sterlig made plans to add onto their house, and Arja came to visit him after Sterlig left for Eydis, telling him how much in love with Sterlig she was and how brave Sterlig was, and how Bjorn would never be like him and just take what he wanted. She'd stood in the middle of his forge, her hands on her hips, looking up at him, daring him to admit he wanted her.

At that, he'd turned her away like a child, and rightfully so. What did a child know of honor? He would not betray his brother. Even though he loved Arja, Bjorn loved her knowing there were some things she didn't understand. A man's honor was a sacred matter.

How could he truly love her, if he couldn't love her honorably?

At the time, there was the matter that she'd promised herself to Sterlig, too. He wouldn't have only compromised himself, but her, too.

So now he was on Eydis, looking for a way to help her—and that meant finding Pyri.

"Watch out!"

Bjorn jumped to the side just as Ephraim brushed past him, carrying a large, empty box. "Sorry," he murmured. "Do you need some help?"

"Not yours." Ephraim scoffed.

Bjorn raised his hands. "I'm sorry I even asked."

"You should know better than most it's better not to accept help from people." Ephraim nodded in the direction Arja and Finnar had headed. "That's how you were forced into this in the first place, isn't it?"

"If I got forced into it, it stands to reason that I was not asked."

"Psh." Ephraim shook his head. "Those who are determined are quick to find a way to accomplish what they want, even if it is by dishonorable means."

Bjorn studied the smaller trader, walking with him as he moved around the port. "Why are you here then? Did someone trick you?"

"I was the second son of a fisherman, back in my country," Ephraim said. He put down the box and sighed. "I was captured when a neighboring nation attacked, and I was sold off as part of the spoils of war. They killed my father and the rest of my family."

"I'm sorry." Bjorn looked down.

"I didn't want to become a fisherman. I was good at changing money. After I was captured, I was sold and eventually, I arrived on Snæland as a thrall for the Thordirsson clan."

"The chieftain?"

"Not the current one." Ephraim gave Bjorn a grim look and pointed to his tattoo. "I am over a hundred years old now."

"Oh, yes. I forgot," Bjorn replied quickly. "Sorry."

Ephraim did not seem to notice his apology, and if he did, he did not care. He continued with his story.

"I was a good sailor, using what my father taught me, so when one of Jarl Thordirsson's sons wanted to go to Eydis, in hopes of re-uniting the lands under one ruler, I went along as a thrall."

"He did not survive when you came here." Bjorn sighed. "The dragon was too powerful."

"Yes, she is," Ephraim agreed. "But it doesn't help when strong men come here expecting to win the kingdom and the hand of Princess Brynja."

Bjorn looked back over toward the castle, surprised to see a glimmer of white light twinkling at the top. He blinked and squinted, trying to see what it was, but it was too hard to see from where he was standing.

"I didn't care for my owner's son. When he came here, he was quickly killed, and I did not have any remorse. I can't speak for how the princess felt, but she was moved enough that she offered us a home here. She had an interest in growing her island's perfumery, and she needed more sailors."

"So you were freed."

"I was freed, and then I was seduced into a different kind of servitude." Ephraim scowled. "I was promised riches and comfort, and after years of serving others, I embraced a chance to be in control of my own destiny. But it turned out to be a curse instead of a gift. It turns out greed is a worse master than man, because greed is not bound by mortal limits."

Ephraim's tattoo glowered with a red aura.

"You've said too much," Bjorn told him.

"You think I don't know that?" Ephraim snapped. "You're lucky Camille has taken a liking to you, and that we've managed to get you here at all. Go now, before I regret my actions even more."

"Where should I go?" Bjorn asked, gesturing to the port around him. "I'd like to get my sword sharpened."

"Doesn't matter where you go, just go," Ephraim told him. "It looks like rain is coming, and you don't want to be outside when it arrives."

Bjorn nodded. "Thank you."

Ephraim glared at him, but he said nothing else. Bjorn took his silence as a kindness, and began walking down the wharf. After looking around carefully, Bjorn headed in the direction of the castle tower, careful to keep one hand on his sword and one hand on the pouch on his belt.

Kyvan's port was much larger, but Bjorn could still spot the usual characters. There were some who were the seasoned hagglers, clearly using everything at their disposal to get a better deal, whether it was on meat or goods. There were fisherman who had already brought in their morning hauls, and gamblers goading those passing by to press their luck. As Bjorn walked by the baker, his stomach ached at the smell, but then another scent caught his attention. It was coming from a small, uphill path, leading away from the port.

Bjorn stepped onto the path and the potency of the smell increased. He followed it up the hill, and tucked away at the side was a small turf house, similar to his family's turf house in Kyvan.

Vines covered the long wall beside the house, and little green bulbs hung between the leaves. As Bjorn walked up to it, a bulb blossomed into a full flower before him.

Bjorn stopped and stared. The flower was large and white, with a small violet stamens in the center, and its fragrance was full of musk and mystery. At once, his mind was filled with images of Arja.

He touched the flower softly, marveling at its design.

It would be a perfect gift for Arja.

A nearby gate opened up in the fence, and an old woman appeared at its entrance. Her hair was intricately braided back, but it was thin and white, and even from where he was standing, he could see the milky white film in her eyes.

"Aren't you going to take it, young man?" The old woman asked, a small cackle in her voice. "There are plenty who wouldn't hesitate to take it. Especially from a harmless old lady like myself."

THE LEGEND OF EYDIS

He took a step back, watching as her blinded eyes followed his movements.

She could still see him, he realized, tightening his hand on his sword. She was not blind; she was a *seidr*.

"Well, that's a new one." The old woman grinned, showing her smile full of missing teeth. "You're not even going to answer me?"

"I don't take things that don't belong to me." Bjorn gave her a courteous nod. "Your flowers are beautiful. I was just admiring them."

"These are Her Highness' favorite blooms, the moonflowers of Eydis," the old woman said. "From them, we make our famous perfume, and our elixir is said to be a gift of pure love."

"I know of its reputation."

The old woman smiled. "But not of its power?"

Bjorn slowly shook his head.

"Good." The older woman cackled. "It's a legendary gift, but legends are full of lies. Our perfume indeed is a gift of pure love, but it never lasts. Its beauty is crushed and pounded and soaked, boiled and steamed into its essence, and then mixed with any number of other items. And then it is sold for a price."

Bjorn was not certain of how to reply, and the old woman just laughed.

"You're a smart man. Some things are only learned through experience. You will see what I mean."

Bjorn looked back at the bloom. "Can I purchase this bloom from you?"

"No." The woman smiled. "But it is my pleasure to give it to you."

Bjorn gave her an amused look. "There is no price when it's a gift, is there?"

"Not when it is given freely, with nothing expected in return." The older woman stepped up next to him and pulled the flower from the vine. "Your wife will love it."

"Thank you." Bjorn smiled down at the moonflower, still thinking of Arja. The *seidr* had called her his wife, and it made him hopeful that she would be right one day, even if it seemed impossible for now.

The woman held out the flower. "Your brother never thought as you do, Bjorn Kyvansson."

Bjorn hesitated for only a second before he took the flower from her. "You're Pyri, aren't you?"

"Yes." She patted his hand. "I have shelter for you."

"Shelter?"

"Outsiders don't stay here long. Not without paying a price." She pointed to her arm, reminding Bjorn of Camille and Ephraim, and the other sailors.

Pyri wore long sleeves, so he couldn't see her tattoo, but Bjorn nodded.

"Thank you," he said again. "I'll be happy to pay you for the trouble."

"There is no payment, and there is no trouble—yet," Pyri said as she headed back into her house. "On the contrary, I've been waiting for your arrival."

"You have?" He put his hand on the pommel and immediately let go. The sword was hot, burning as if it were angry, and it glowed a darker green than from before.

Is it because of Pyri?

"Come with me," Pyri said, waving her arm. "It will be all right."

Bjorn didn't move. "What about Arja?"

"She'll be here before the rain falls." Pyri smirked, clearly enjoying Bjorn's confusion.

"How do I know this isn't a trick?" Bjorn couldn't explain it, but he felt as though he was being tested, and he did not appreciate the thought.

"It's not." Pyri pointed to the pouch on his belt. "Your mother's gift is protecting you."

Bjorn pulled out his mother's crucifix. The golden cross looked no different than from before. There was no aura or glow on it, nothing to show a spell of protection around it or its chain.

"I don't see anything." When he held it up to Pyri, she nodded in understanding of his unspoken question.

"Your mother's prayers are not able to be seen, nor is the hand of God," Pyri explained. "But their power and protection remain steadfast in love, so long as you keep it and trust in it."

"Why does my sword glow then?" Bjorn asked. "And the tattoos on Camille and Ephraim and the others?"

"Love is not the only source of power. Surely you of all people know that."

Thunder rumbled in the distance, as if to agree with her.

"Come," Pyri said. "I'll show you to your quarters for the evening."

Seeing no other option, Bjorn tucked his mother's cross back inside its bag, and followed after Pyri, hoping Camille had been right about her.

❖   ❖   ❖

"Well, there's nothing over this way." Arja pulled her shield down from her back and dropped it onto the ground near a large rock.

She'd taken the morning to climb halfway up the mountain just off to the side of Eydis' port, the one opposite to the castle tower. Finnar lugged himself behind her, and Arja was glad he was in better spirits since leaving the ship. He was still less cheerful than his usual self, but as he talked and joked with her, it was almost like their hikes into Kyvan, though Eydis was nothing like home.

She glanced around. The cove that housed the fishing boats and the *Sea Serpent* was protected by a surrounding ring of hills and mountains, resting in the middle of them like a pearl trapped in an oyster. At the center of the island was a large field, dotted with flowers and the people working to gather them. The mountains bordered the small city, almost another type dragon, only made of nature and rocks rather than teeth and scales.

"You mean we walked all this way over here for nothing?" Finnar groaned.

"You know we're supposed to look for Pyri. I thought for sure she'd be hiding on the opposite end of the island from how Camille talked about her."

"Well, she doesn't," Finnar snorted. "No one seems to live that far from the port, except for the princess. It's not like Kyvan, where there's plenty of land left to farm."

"Stop complaining. Maybe Bjorn found her."

"Yes, and maybe he's already at the castle, fighting for Brynja's hand and the freedom of the island."

Arja bit her lip, tasting the memory of Bjorn's kiss from earlier. "Don't say that."

Finnar narrowed his eyes at her, but Arja turned her back to him, studying the beauty of the island instead of confronting her brother.

Eydis had always been shrouded in mystery, and despite their reason for coming, Arja was excited she was finally getting to see it for herself. The island was home to the famous perfume trade, and rumors spoke of great ogres and small trolls, and there were stories of warriors that made it to the halls of Valhalla who returned to visit the island.

During their afternoon trek, she'd seen no evidence of such, but she had seen a lot of wary eyes look as the clouds rolled in and began to darken.

"There's something strange about this place, but I can't quite name it," she said.

"I'd rather you didn't." Finnar slumped to the ground. They had walked through the small port, looking through the merchant shops and small farms nearby. Afterward, finding no one interested in talking, they'd hiked up into the outskirts of the town. "With how things have been lately, you'd likely summon a demon."

"You've been talking to Bjorn, I see." Arja sighed. "More concerned with demons than dragons."

"Both are bad, in my estimation." Finnar's blue eyes darkened as he glanced back toward the island port. "This whole place is bad. This is where Sterlig died."

"Here? On this mountain?" Arja straightened, unnerved at the thought.

"No, not here, specifically. Just here. On Eydis." Finnar shook his head. He pointed to the tower castle. "There's a door near the bottom of the tower, and behind the mountain's shadow, there's a place where men have battled the dragon on land. Sterlig went there while Jon and I were too scared to even move. We saw him fight the dragon and disappear. Later, the princess tossed his sword out of her tower, expressing her sympathies for his death."

"There was nothing else?"

"The dragon eats the rest." Finnar winced. "I've seen it in my nightmares, and I'd rather drown than be eaten."

Arja came over and sat next to him. "You shouldn't have to suffer for Sterlig's mistake."

"So I suffer for yours instead?" Finnar gave her a teasing smirk.

Arja punched his shoulder. "That's not funny."

"But it's the truth, isn't it?" Finnar rolled his eyes. "Ah, well. I know you well, Arja, and I know you wouldn't hesitate to suffer for me in my place, even if it means your life."

Arja eyed him skeptically. "But?"

"There's not really anything else for that part." Finnar's expression darkened. "But for all you'd like to believe you can take down the world without a second thought, you can't do this. Not even Sterlig could do this."

Arja laughed. "Oh, no. Don't tell me the great Sterlig Kyvansson wasn't able to fell the dragon of Eydis. Not after the other legendary pillage and plunders he'd undertaken."

"Arja." Finnar met her gaze. "You shouldn't be laughing."

She sighed. "I know. But you know as well as I do, Finn, that most of his exploits were exaggerated. And he enjoyed embellishing things for a willing crowd. Or even an unwilling one."

She thought of how he'd talked of his love for her, and how much he wanted to marry her and have a large family with her, just as her father did with her mother. He never seemed to realize or care how much his daydreams never fit into her own life, or even her own nature.

Finnar let out a huff. "You shouldn't laugh. For all Sterlig's flaws, you've brought Bjorn into it now."

Abruptly, Arja stood back up. "I think we've had enough of a rest. Especially if you're talking this much."

"Arja, wait. I saw you and Bjorn earlier—"

"So?" She didn't want to talk about Bjorn with her brother. Anything Finnar said would only make her feel more awkward. She'd told herself she

THE LEGEND OF EYDIS

enjoyed getting a good deal out of Camille for the price of the trip, and it was welcoming not having to deal with unwanted advances from the other men. Having Bjorn around to dissuade others was a relief, and it had given her time to prepare herself for fighting the dragon.

Except she had barely used the time for that, preferring instead to think of Bjorn and his kisses, and how he'd allowed her to sleep next to him to soothe her nightmares. She relived those moments before sleep, almost as if it was a dream on its own as she felt his loving caress, his hand running over her hair and down her cheek. She thought of slipping into sleep at last, and an uncomfortable ache in her belly wondered if he would be as kind to his children. Arja had been able to sleep, but she woke up feeling twice as burdened at the thought; she was robbing another woman of a good husband and unborn children of a loving father—all so she could put her brothers' fears to rest and bury her own guilt.

"You're not being fair to him, you know."

"He was the one who didn't want to marry me," Arja scoffed. "That's why I came here in the first place."

"Arja."

"What?" She threw up her hands, exasperated. "Finn, I swear by the gods—"

"I know you love him. Can't you just admit it?"

"No." Arja pushed back the sting of tears, adamant that Finnar wouldn't make her cry. "No, and I'm not going to talk about this with you anymore. You wouldn't understand."

"Well, I definitely won't, if you can't tell me the truth."

"Ha. This is coming from someone who never bothered to mention to me how Sterlig forgot all about me when he arrived here on the island." Arja put her hands on her hips, and Finnar blanched.

"So you were awake then," he murmured. "I didn't want to hurt you, Arja."

"I wish you would've told me. I would've felt better that he'd died."

"You don't mean that."

"Yes, I do," she snapped. "I know it's horrible to think that, but I do."

Finnar said nothing as he came up beside her. He wrapped his arm around her shoulder and ran his hand over her hand affectionately.

Arja softened at his kindness. Finnar had always been a good brother to her. She knew that he'd hidden the truth from her to protect her, just as she'd wanted to save him from his nightmares.

His comfort made her feel better, but she also felt worse, knowing she didn't deserve it.

"I still don't see what this has to do with Bjorn," Finnar said. "But you should tell him the truth, Arja."

"I can't." Arja glanced around, almost expecting Sterlig's ghost to be behind her, taunting her and leering at her over her fate. She held out her hands, palms up, in a gesture of defeat. "I can't tell Bjorn the truth. He'll never love me if I do—but I can't let him love me without telling him, either."

"Telling him what?"

"Nothing!"

"Sounds like something much more than nothing." Finnar crossed his arms over his chest as he blocked her way.

A new voice spoke up from off to the side. "It would be something, if your nothing would wake up the dragon."

Both Arja and Finnar stepped back. Arja started to reach for her sword when a small child stepped forward.

It was a young girl, wearing a white dress. Her hair was dark and fine, and her large eyes were the color of honey and shimmered with the last of the sunlight. Pure white slippers stuck out from underneath her billowing skirts.

"Who are you?" Arja asked. She stopped reaching for her sword, but something still tugged at her mind. After a moment, she realized it was the first time she'd seen a child on the island.

"My name is Ana." The little girl gave Arja a quick curtsey. "I've come to greet you."

"Why?"

"It's a tradition for me and Lady Pyri," Ana said. "We like to meet those who come to visit Eydis. She's requested that I bring you to her."

"Pyri?" Arja looked over at Finnar, who looked stricken. "That's the lady we were supposed to meet. Lead the way, Ana."

The little girl nodded. "This way."

Finnar grabbed her arm.

"Arja."

She shrugged out of his grip. "What?"

"I recognize her," Finnar whispered. "She was the one with the princess before. She's the one who handed me and Jon Sterlig's sword."

"That was Bjorn's sword."

"Does that really matter now?" Finnar pointed to the girl, who was kneeling in the dirt, playing, as she waited for them. "She works for Princess Brynja."

"But she said she'd take us to Pyri," Arja said. "What's the harm in just following her? She's only a child. And if you've seen her with the princess, she's not going to need protection from the dragon."

"We will, though."

"It's only a matter of time before we meet the dragon anyway. Now, come."

Finnar rolled his eyes, but he made no other objections as Ana lead them back down into the port area, all while the sky darkened. Mist started to roll in from the cove, and soon Arja struggled to

THE LEGEND OF EYDIS

keep Ana in her sight as they walked through the thinning crowds.

Arja watched as Ana playfully brushed up against different vendors, surprising them. Some of them shook their heads while others cursed, but none of them chastised Ana or tried to stop her as she moved throughout the market.

"She certainly seems lively," Finnar grumbled to Arja, as Ana swapped the signs for different fish.

"She's definitely enjoying herself," Arja agreed. "It's a good thing she's not one of our siblings. I would've punished her for her silliness."

"Now you know how I felt when you would follow me around all the time."

Arja nudged him lightly and then hurried to keep up with Ana, who seemed to move through the port much more easily. As Arja watched, Ana slipped in and out of people's way, laughing as she nearly tripped many of them.

None of the people seemed to notice her.

Arja frowned, watching Ana more carefully. It wasn't until they reached the trail out of the port that she noticed it.

"Finn." Arja stopped short, reaching out her arm to block him from following. "She's not leaving any footprints."

"Huh?"

"Look." Arja rolled her eyes. Finnar was nearly out of breath and clearly grateful for the pause in their journey. She pointed down at the ground. Arja's footsteps were clear and defined in the dirt, but there was no sign Ana had been walking there just a moment ago.

Finnar shrugged. "So? She's a small child."

"This is strange," Arja said. She studied the faces of those she passed in the streets. There were plenty of them who were busy, talking in the street with the vendors, buying and exchanging goods; but as she really looked at them, they all had a deadened look in their eyes. "Something is wrong here."

"You're not just figuring that out now, are you?" Finnar sighed.

"I told you. That girl works for the princess. We are only going to find trouble following her."

"She's the only lead we have," Arja said. "And if you think about it, Camille works for the princess, too, but he was still able to bring us and tell us more about the legend of Eydis. Maybe this little girl's like that, too."

Finnar sighed. "I don't know. She's—"

"Tired of waiting for you," Ana said, smoothly interrupting him as she suddenly appeared behind them.

As Arja and Finnar looked at her with surprised looks on their faces, Ana giggled. "You two are silly. I wish I had a brother or sister like you."

"You do?" Arja asked. "You're an only child?"

"I'll trade you," Finnar said with a snort, making Ana laugh again.

"No, I'm the only child my father has," Ana said. The smile on her face disappeared. "He's dead now."

"Oh, I'm sorry," Arja said. She was still unsure of Ana, but she was used to comforting her younger brothers, and it was natural for her to soften as Ana looked away.

"Yes, he died a long time ago," Ana said. "But I know he loved me very much."

"I'm sure he did," Arja agreed. "You're very pretty."

Ana wriggled her nose. "There's more to loving someone than being pretty."

"Well, of course there is," Arja said. "But we've just met, haven't we? So I know you're pretty, and I know you're also helpful, since you're taking us to Lady Pyri."

"That's true." Ana seemed mollified. "My father always did like it when I would listen to him. He always wanted me to be a good girl and listen to him. And he was always right."

Arja smiled, thinking of her own father, and how he was always so kind to her mother. Ana's affection for her father comforted Arja.

Perhaps she's not as strange as I thought. Looking around, and seeing the empty stares surrounding her, Arja wondered if her discomfort was more due to Eydis. It was a cursed island, living with its own dragon protector, and that alone had to explain why normal things—like children—seemed odd to her.

Even if Ana was still the only child on the island.

Arja bit her lip. It was possible the island and the girl were *both* strange, and she would do well to remember that.

"Arja! Finn!"

Arja heard Bjorn call to her, and she felt a rush of relief. Even if Ana was a ghost or an illusion, she knew Bjorn was real.

She hurried forward into the parting mist, just as lightning dashed through the clouds. She found herself in front of a small house covered with vines and flowers.

"Bjorn."

Arja saw Bjorn standing near the house's entrance. Beside him was Ana and another old woman, who waved at them, gesturing for them to come quickly.

"Hurry," the old woman said, opening the door. "You don't have much time. The dragon comes out when it rains, looking for her next prey. You need to hide."

As raindrops fell on her face, Arja didn't hesitate. She hurried into the house with Finnar at her heels, just as a loud roar of thunder—or perhaps a dragon—crashed through the skies. Once they were inside, Arja stared at the storm, mesmerized by the swirling winds.

"We made it, thank the Allfather." Bjorn shut the door behind them, just as the rain began to pour. "We're fortunate Lady Pyri has opened her home to us."

"Pyri?" Arja looked over at the older woman, who smiled graciously at Bjorn. "Camille's Pyri?"

"Yes, I'm Camille's Pyri." She gestured toward the storm outside. "And I welcome the chance to shelter you while you're here to visit the island. I will have dinner ready soon, too."

"Well, I'll agree to that," Finnar said. "I'm tired of rain and water, but I'm more tired of dried fish and rotting fruit."

The old woman looked over at him. "I didn't anticipate you would return, Finnar Freysson."

"I hope it's not because you thought I would die first."

Pyri gave him a small laugh. "I suppose you didn't notice my house on your previous trip."

"I remember your face," Finnar said. "But not much else."

"I'm sure you remember your friend telling you what a witch I was."

Finnar shuffled his feet with a guilty look on his face. "Some things are better forgotten."

Eager to avoid talking about Sterlig, Arja looked around. That was when she noticed Ana was gone.

She walked around, glancing at some of the other rooms in the house. "Where is Ana?"

"Who's Ana?" Bjorn asked.

"That little girl. Didn't you see her? She was with us," Arja said.

"There's no need to worry." Pyri waved her hand in a dismissive gesture. "She left."

"Ana left?" Arja repeated. "In the rain? But she's just a child."

"She's safe from the dragon." Pyri tugged on her arm. "Now, all of you, come over here to the fire. I'll make some tea, and perhaps we can discuss Sterlig's death, and how you will defeat this dragon of ours here on Eydis."

Arja felt the blood drain from her face, but she nodded. "Yes, that's a good idea."

"I won't say no to food," Finnar said, already moving toward the warmth of the fire pit in Pyri's house. "Got anything fresh?"

"Watch your manners, Finn," Bjorn said with a small laugh, before he took Arja's hand.

Arja squeezed his hand back, feeling the old blisters and callouses on his palm from his years of working as a blacksmith. She thought of Sterlig, and his father, and all the other people from Kyvan who had given him grief, even herself. Bjorn had born their carelessness and neglect and stubbornness with strength and even graciousness.

Finnar was right. She loved him.

Arja remembered her own words to Camille before. How could she resist Bjorn indeed?

She was right to have trusted him with her fate. But as they sat down at Pyri's table, she was still not sure if it was enough that she could trust him with the truth.

THE LEGEND OF EYDIS

14

❖   ❖   ❖

Despite the raging thunder and lightning outside, it was warm and cozy inside Pyri's house.

Arja watched Pyri expertly host their small party with wonder, given the older woman's blinded eyes and age. In some ways, Pyri reminded Arja of her mother as she poured tea for them. Her movements were sure and graceful, like a mother's should be.

"Here we are." Pyri smiled as she set out bread and cheese with their meal. Arja recognized some of the items from the cargo hold of the *Sea Serpent*.

"It should be fresh. Camille knows I have a fondness for *hangikjöt*," Pyri said. "As you've seen for yourself now, we don't have a lot of farms on the island. We have enough from the sea to get by, but I am certain it was our love for proper meat that drove us to begin trading with the outside world again. Working with the perfumery was just a good front for us to present our request to Princess Brynja."

"That was how you met Camille, and Ephraim, and the others, wasn't it?" Bjorn asked. "Princess Brynja opened trade and other nations started coming here."

Pyri nodded. "Camille and I have been good friends since he was brought here. The princess freed him, along with the others, and they have been serving here faithfully ever since."

"I imagine a lot of them are eager to see the princess freed from the dragon. Many of them seem very loyal to her," Arja said. After all, Camille had risked his life to tell her to find Pyri, and the dragon's blood in his tattoo had caused him pain.

Pyri shrugged. "She is a very beautiful and tragic figure. Many are sympathetic to her cause."

"That's understandable," Bjorn said, giving Arja a teasing smirk.

She frowned at him and nudged him under the table. Now that she knew Sterlig had abandoned her memory in hopes of winning the princess—and now that she worried there was a possibility Bjorn would do so, too—Arja did not want to indulge in any jests.

"The legend of Brynja the Bride, added to the promise of a kingdom, and now the treasure of a successful perfume trade have brought many suitors to the island. They all hope to be her champion," Pyri said.

"They all are blinded by her beauty," Finnar said.

"But there's more to love than beauty," Arja said, giving him a small smile as she repeated Ana's earlier words.

"And they all died," Bjorn said.

Arja huffed. "Yes, like Sterlig did."

Bjorn and Finn looked over at her in surprise, and Arja quickly cleared her throat. "Sadly, I mean."

She took a drink of tea, glad the mug hid her face.

When she was finished, Pyri looked at her with an amused expression on her face.

"Perhaps you are right about the sad part," Pyri said. There was enough of an edge to her voice that Arja knew she was teasing her. "But he did manage to do something that was quite different from the others."

"He did?" Arja put down her cup.

Pyri turned to Bjorn and held out her gnarled hands. "May I see your sword, please?"

Bjorn nodded and pulled it out of its sheath. Arja watched as he handed it to Pyri, who examined it carefully.

"It seems he's settled down some since he came in here," Pyri said.

"He?" Arja frowned. She looked down at the sword, thinking of how she'd seen it glow before.

"He died after he managed to cause the dragon to bleed its true blood," Pyri said. "It's never happened before. Some of his spirit is unable to rest, thanks to the power of the dragon blood."

Arja and Bjorn exchanged an uneasy glance.

"So he's … still alive?" Arja asked. She hated how her heart began pounding between her ears, as she thought back to all those moments when she'd been with Bjorn and his sword.

"No." Pyri shook her head. "Like the residents on this island, he is unable to die completely. But he is still dead."

"I don't understand," Bjorn said, his voice sounding strangled in his throat.

"I think you do," Pyri corrected him. "You know your brother better than anyone else, don't you?"

Bjorn went silent, while Arja fought back the urge to take his sword and toss it out the window.

"I do," she said, standing up. "He's the one who's been giving us nightmares, isn't he? I've seen the aura around the sword. I thought it was the curse of Eydis, but it turns out it was just Sterlig, wasn't it?"

"Arja." Bjorn reached for her. "It's—"

"It's just like him to do this." Arja gritted her teeth. She felt the urge to hit something, and her fists clenched in fury. "He's probably happy we've been suffering all this time."

Bjorn stood up and took hold of her hand. "It's all right. If the dragon blood is what is keeping his spirit alive, then we will be able to put him to rest once the dragon is dead. Right?"

He looked over at Pyri, who nodded.

THE LEGEND OF EYDIS

"So you were right," Bjorn said softly. "We will have to slay the dragon, if we're going to fix everything."

At the gentle certainty of his statement, Arja wanted to hit him. Bjorn was in danger, all because she'd been tricked by Sterlig.

No, they were all in danger, she corrected herself, but she didn't care what happened to her anymore. It was all her fault they were here.

Pyri stood up and handed Bjorn back his sword. "He didn't like me at first, when he ran into me. He was quite careless with my blooms, you know, and I didn't appreciate his ego."

"That sounds like Sterlig," Bjorn murmured, and Arja had to choke down half an angry laugh.

"Yes, it does sound like him. He's causing the most amount of inconvenience to people, even with his death. If he wasn't dead already, I'd kill him," Arja scoffed.

"Arja." Bjorn came up beside her again.

She avoided his gaze as she shook her head. "My brothers have nearly killed themselves because of him."

"Not quite."

Bjorn and Arja looked over at Pyri, who returned to her chair at the table.

"What do you mean?"

"It's not Sterlig who's trying to kill me and Jon." Finnar leaned back in his chair. "There's another power at work, too, isn't there, Pyri?"

"With the dragon blood on the sword, you've been cursed since it came back to you," Pyri explained.

Finnar nodded. "That was my general feeling on the matter, but it's nice to hear it confirmed."

Arja eyed the sword again. "So the only way to defeat the curse and help my brothers—"

"And yourself," Finnar reminded her.

"Is to kill the dragon," Bjorn finished. He slid the sword back into its sheath.

"Yes." Pyri nodded. "But you already knew that, didn't you?"

"I did." Arja crossed her arms over her chest.

"But the question is how we defeat it now," Bjorn said. "If Sterlig managed to make it bleed its true blood, but he still lost, then there must be something else we need to do."

"There is, and it starts with discovering the truth," Pyri said.

Arja ignored the pointed look Finnar gave her.

"You can tell us that, can't you, Pyri?" Bjorn asked. "You're not bound to the dragon at all, are you?"

Arja glanced over at Pyri and noticed that Finnar did, too.

"He's right," Pyri agreed. She held up her arm, and Arja frowned.

"She doesn't have a tattoo," Bjorn explained.

"I am protected from the dragon's magic," Pyri said. "That's also why your brother's spirit has been resting while we're in here."

Outside of the house, thunder crackled and lightning flashed in a deadly dance. Bjorn and Arja gasped, while Finnar turned away from the windows. Arja ignored the small whimper that escaped him.

"It seems the dragon is especially mad tonight. But never fear. We should use this time to rest." Pyri stood up again and turned to look at her. "You haven't had a good night sleep in some time, have you, Arja Freydottir? It's time to rest, and I've prepared the perfect room for you and your husband. I have a nice room for your brother, too."

The last of the chill in the air dispersed as she blushed. "Are you sure—"

Pyri nodded. "You are safe, here in my house. The dragon won't find you, and the storm will slow once she returns to her nest under the island."

"We could all use some rest," Bjorn agreed. "Thank you for your help. You've given us a lot to think about."

Arja kept her complaints to herself. Pyri had told them plenty, but it hadn't changed their mission at all—not in her eyes, anyway.

THE LEGEND OF EYDIS

Arja suddenly realized it was possibly her last night with Bjorn, the last night she might be alive with him, she fell silent. She could sleep through nightmares over Sterlig's fate, now she was living through nightmares where she lost Bjorn. She felt her heart pulsate in pure anguish at the thought, and her head began to throb with guilt and anger and longing.

"Come along." Pyri motioned them to follow her. "Tomorrow will be a long day for you."

Tomorrow would be a long day, Arja thought. But it would be a long night, too.

❖　　❖　　❖

Bjorn watched as Arja slept on next to him, wondering at the beauty of her features. He had no idea how many hours had passed since Pyri left them, and it was still raining as he lay there, looking at his would-be bride, but he felt rested and more alive than ever.

Now that they were alone—truly alone—he thought about playfully kissing her awake, finding some excuse to pretend he had good cause to present themselves as married. He could say Pyri was in the hall, or some other nonsense, and he'd kissed her to make sure their story remained intact.

He doubted she would believe him, and he doubted he would be able to stop kissing her if he started.

Arja could be the very devil when she was awake, but she was every bit the angel when she slept. Bjorn watched her with unbound adoration, taking in her even breathing, her pert little nose flaring, the little murmurings she muttered as she shifted across the bed.

After Pyri showed them to their room, Arja had gone to bed almost immediately. She'd given him some excuse about the rain making her tired, but Bjorn had a feeling she was more desperate to avoid him, especially after Pyri mentioned Sterlig.

He inched closer to her on the bed, lost in wonder. It wouldn't be the first time someone had chosen Sterlig over him. Even death had not managed to dislodge Sterlig from his father's favor. Bjorn was used to that from others as well, having grown up hearing others ask why his mother was teaching him to read and his uncle was training him to be a blacksmith, all while his father taught Sterlig how to go viking and be a warrior.

But Arja was different. He touched her hair, enjoying the feel of the soft tresses between his fingers.

The rest of the world could choose Sterlig over him a million times and he wouldn't care, so long as he had Arja. And after Pyri's talk with them earlier, he had enough hope that Arja would choose him.

He glanced up at the small cup above their pallet. The moonflower Pyri had given him had blossomed in the darkness, and its scent fluttered around the room.

Arja shifted on the bed beside him.

"Bjorn." She whispered his name in her sleep. When she reached for him a moment later, Bjorn felt himself fall into a temptation he couldn't resist.

He leaned over and pressed his lips against hers, wrapping his arm around her and pulling her closer to him.

Her eyes blinked open, and then she closed them again as she kissed him back. Her hands ran through his hair and down his back.

"Bjorn." This time, his name escaped with a small moan of longing and passion.

Bjorn fell against her. Her lips were soft and full. He felt like the sky, finally touching the ground and finding it full of flowers, and he was consumed by a flood of sensations as he held her.

"Bjorn, please." Arja broke away and tried to slide away from him. "This is too much."

"What's wrong?" Panic stirred inside of him. "Don't you like my kisses, Arja?"

"I do. I mean, it's not that," Arja said. "This just … feels too real. I know you don't really want to marry me—"

"By the Allfather, Arja, that's enough." His voice was sharp and impatient as he rolled over on top of her, cradling her face in his hands before he kissed her, desperately and roughly. "Of course I want to."

"You do?" Arja pressed her hands into his chest, pushing him away enough she could peer up at him.

"Yes." He looked her squarely in the eye as he took her bottom lip in his teeth, watching as her gaze blurred over with pleasure.

"I thought you said no man in his right mind would ever want to marry me." Arja trembled as he kissed her neck.

"I have never been in my right mind around you."

"You said I was a spiteful shrew."
"You are, but I still love you." He was breathless as he kissed her again, sliding his lips over hers as he took hold of her wrists and pinned her underneath him. His heart pounded in his chest as she arched against him. "I've tried to love you in an honorable manner, but I can't resist you right now."

"You love me?" Arja frowned. "This doesn't seem right."

"It is."

"It could be Pyri's magic," Arja whispered.

"It's not." Bjorn let go of her and reached for his pouch where he'd placed his mother's crucifix. "Pyri says my mother's prayers have protected me.

It's in keeping with the missionary teachings, so I have no reason to doubt her."

"Your mother's prayers?" Arja faltered briefly, before she touched the cross in Bjorn's hand. "I guess that makes sense. She loves you so much."

"She loves you, too." Bjorn placed the cross in Arja's hand, and then pressed it into her palm. He had nothing more precious to give her as a sign of his devotion. "She told me if I wanted to marry you, I would have her blessing."

Arja's fingers tightened around the necklace. "She did?"

"Yes." Bjorn leaned over and kissed her softly. "She knew I loved you."

Arja stilled. "Wait. Bjorn, there's something I have to tell you."

He sighed, before he pulled away from her and sat on the edge of the bed. "This is about Sterlig, isn't it?"

"Yes." Arja closed her eyes. "I—"

"You still love him."

"What?" Arja's eyes snapped open, blazing with anger. "No. No, that's not it at all."

It was Bjorn's turn to look confused. "What is it, then?"

"It's … it's my fault he's dead." Arja slid back from him and covered her face in her hands.

"I know he said he would go for you, but that doesn't mean his death is your fault." Bjorn moved

THE LEGEND OF EYDIS

over beside her and pressed a small kiss on her forehead. "You don't need to blame yourself."

"Don't be like him, Bjorn, please. Sterlig didn't know me at all, but I know you do." Arja grimaced. "He thought I chased after him because I was always eager to see you and Jon and Finn, and he thought I would get past my fear of having children. He said I would make him a good wife, and he would make me a better husband than you."

Bjorn said nothing.

She looked away. "He did everything he could to make sure I knew you weren't the better choice between the two of you. I hated how he would talk about you. He told me before he left that he'd steal your sword to show me how if he wanted something, he would just take it, and that included what belonged to you."

"That doesn't matter," Bjorn said, standing up. "I expected that of him."

"Stop that," Arja scoffed. "You don't get it, Bjorn. *I* belong to you."

"No you don't."

She jumped up and came to him, flattening her palms across his chest as she pushed him into the wall behind him. "By the Allfather, Bjorn, *yes, I do*."

Bjorn held onto her shoulders. "So you didn't love Sterlig?"

"Of course I didn't love him," Arja snapped. "It didn't stop him from asking me to marry him. I kept ignoring him or teasing him, and then refusing him directly when he began berating me. And when he got rough with it—"

"Wait." Bjorn felt anger burn into him. "Sterlig didn't hurt you, did he?"

"No," Arja huffed. She stepped back from him and turned away. "But he certainly learned a few words from your father. And after he started insulting you, I had enough."

Bjorn shook his head. Everything she was saying ran together. Carefully, he pulled back from Arja and sat down on the bed as she paced.

"I said my father bought perfume from Eydis for my mother, and if Sterlig was going to marry me, he should do more than that, and if he really was so strong, he would slay the dragon." Arja looked down at her hands. "You've said it yourself that words and swords both have their uses, and I'm the reason he went to Eydis."

Bjorn clenched his fists together.

"Once he agreed, he started bragging to everyone who had ears I was going to marry him. I didn't correct him at the time, figuring when he failed to get to Eydis, or he changed his mind, I could keep him away from me by threatening to tell the truth. I didn't realize … I didn't think he'd actually go."

"What did you think would happen?" Bjorn stood up, exasperated. How irresponsible could she be?

No wonder she wanted to get rid of her nightmares so badly.

Then there was Jon and Finnar. And his mother had suffered, and his father was drinking himself senseless, all because of Sterlig's foolishness—and Arja's scheming.

"I wasn't thinking!" Arja threw up her hands, flushing over furiously. "He just made me so angry, so I said I would marry you if he didn't succeed. That was when he started planning his trip."

"But what about that day after he left, when you told me how you loved him—"

"Oh, Bjorn, please. It was *you* I wanted." Arja's voice nearly broke at her confession. "I was trying to get you to elope with me while he was away. You really are more honorable than anyone else I know, Bjorn. It makes you dense when it comes to women. And if you'd just stood up for yourself and asked for my hand sooner, none of this would've happened."

Bjorn backed away from her and frowned. "You're blaming me for Sterlig's death, too?"

"What? No … No, I'm not." Arja shook her head fiercely. "No, I'm trying to tell you I love you—that I've always loved you. And I've always been here for you, Bjorn. Not Sterlig."

"Arja." Bjorn ran a hand through his hair. He could barely speak, he was so angry. "Do you realize how much trouble you've caused?"

"Of course I do." Arja crossed her arms in front of her chest. "I never wanted to tell you, either. And I never thought you really felt the same way about me that I felt about you. Why didn't you tell me?"

"I won't be your replacement for Sterlig," Bjorn snapped. "And I wouldn't just take you because I wanted to. That's something my brother would do, but not me. I guess I get to share in his punishment regardless, now that we're here."

"I didn't plan for things to go like this."

"You didn't plan at all!" Bjorn felt the last of his patience disappear at her foolishness. "Not with this, and not with Sterlig. And we're not the only ones affected by this, Arja. What about my mother?"

"I'm sorry." Arja's eyes swelled with angry tears.

Bjorn headed toward the door. "You and Sterlig were perfect for each other. You both live for the pleasure that comes from ruining my life."

"I didn't mean to cause all this, I swear. And I'll do anything to make it up to you. You can have me, if that's what you want."

"What?" Bjorn whirled . "You think I'll forgive you if we—"

"Yes. You want me, don't you?"

Bjorn was taken aback by her question, and even more so by her candor. "Arja, please—"

"Don't you?"

"Of course I do, but—

"Then you can take me. Please," she begged, pressing her lips against his in a fervent kiss. "Please, Bjorn. I want you, too."

"Stop." Bjorn felt the temptation to stay with her. But a moment later, he pushed her away.

She stumbled back and fell to the bed. He could see the shock and heartache in her eyes, and a tear slipped down her cheek.

"This isn't right, Arja." He struggled to keep his voice down, belatedly recalling there were other people in the house, and they could likely hear him. "I don't want you like *this*, Arja. Don't you understand?"

This was just like before, he thought. There was so much she didn't seem to understand. He couldn't just sleep with her, or marry her, and then everything would go away.

And that was only part of his frustration with her.

How could she treat her body with such disdain, that she would offer herself to him as an object he could use to temper his anger? No matter how much he might have wanted her, he wanted her heart first. Not her contrition or begrudging acceptance. He wouldn't take her body as a form of retribution for her sins against him and his family, either. Arja's offer only promised emptiness and temporal relief from their current situation.

They were still stuck on Eydis, and her brothers were still having nightmares, and Camille and his crew were still bound to the dragon of Eydis.

So much depended on them now, and like before, they had no real plan.

"Bjorn?" Arja whispered his name. This time, it was sharp and harsh against the silence in the room. He knew she was asking if he could forgive her, and he didn't have an answer for her yet.

He shook his head. "I need some air."

That was all he could manage to say as he pushed past her. As he was leaving the room, he saw his sword leaning against the doorframe.

It was almost like that night, the one before he agreed to journey to Kyvan with Arja. He picked it up carefully, and then he walked out the door, shutting it firmly behind him.

Bjorn did not know where he was going, but he was soon outside of Pyri's house, lost in his own thoughts.

15

Arja sat on the bed, forcing herself to remain calm.

She'd had her time to curl up and cry, but nothing had changed.

Bjorn had not come back.

Once he'd walked out of the room, she crumpled, falling down onto the bed, staring at the door, hoping and willing Bjorn to come back to her.

He had such patience with his overbearing father, and he'd endured so much suffering at the hands of his pompous brother, and the general dismissal from others in Kyvan. Bjorn was a good and honorable man, and the Bjorn she knew was also a reliable and gracious man.

She was certain he would forgive her.

She was less certain as the hours began to pass, and there was still no sign of him.

Arja held onto the crucifix; she wore it knowing she would never be worthy of it, but she would never willingly rid herself of it, either. She sat on the bed, turning it over in her fingers as she prayed, though it was hard to say if any god would hear her prayer.

She had known the truth, and she had kept it hidden from him. Honor demanded her honesty, and love demanded her bravery. She had given them both in hopes of forgiveness and then acceptance, but the very idea of mercy was a divine one, and one that seemed out of her mortal reach.

It was still dark when Arja heard a knock at the door.

"Bjorn?" His name escaped her as a whimper as she looked at the door.

"Arja? Bjorn?"

At the sound of Finnar's voice, Arja's heart fell once more. She exhaled sharply before tucking the necklace back under her tunic.

"What is it?" Arja called back to Finnar, irritated. The last thing she needed now was another accusation.

"I found something."

There was no easy way to get rid of him, so Arja grabbed her boots. "Coming."

After one last moment of weakness, she took a deep, steadying breath, straightened her shoulders, and opened the door.

"What is it?" she asked.

Her brother looked past her into the room. "Where's Bjorn?"

"Why?" Arja crossed her arms.

"I told you. I've found something, and I wanted to show it to both of you. Why are you getting so defensive?"

THE LEGEND OF EYDIS

"I didn't sleep well," Arja lied, before she pushed past him. "You'll have to show Bjorn later. He's not in the room right now."

"Where is he then? He didn't leave the house, did he?"

"He said he needed some air." Arja dragged him behind her, doing her best to ignore the concern she heard in Finnar's voice. "Tell me where we're going, will you?"

"You and Bjorn didn't get into a lover's spat last night, did you?" Finnar eyed her more carefully, and then slowly grinned. "Or did you perhaps—"

"If you say one more word about me and Bjorn, I'll drag you out of here by the hair and feed you the dragon myself," Arja snapped.

Finnar arched his brow at her vitriol. "Well, that's doubtful," Finnar retorted, but he still took a cautious step back.

Arja swallowed the lump in her throat. "Keep it up, and you'll see how likely it actually is."

Finnar rolled his eyes, but he said nothing as he led Arja through Pyri's house.

He opened another door and Arja briefly forgot about her troubles.

Outside of Pyri's house, the ground was nearly covered in vines and moss.

"What time is it?" Arja asked, looking up at the sky. It was still dark and dreary, and even if it was past sunrise she wouldn't have been able to tell for certain.

"It's still morning yet," Finnar said, looking at the clouds. "Pyri was up and headed into town to see Camille. I think she likes him quite a bit."

Arja looked down at the ground. "Well, I hope she's happy at least."

"Don't pout, Arja." Finnar sighed. "Come this way."

A small hilltop of black dirt and ash was in the middle of Pyri's yard. While the rest of the yard was covered in dew and dotted with small buds, this small area was barren. The smell of the flowers masked the remnant of blood and fire, but even the potency of the plants surrounding it couldn't hide the certainty of death.

"What is it, Finnar?" Arja asked, looking around. She shivered, suddenly uneasy.

"I think it's a grave."

Arja and Finnar exchanged an uneasy look. There was no need for graves on Eydis, given the dragon's curse that took death away from those who were tattooed with her blood.

Arja stepped closer to the small mound. There was a stone at the top, one that was inscribed with an eagle. Finnar was right—it was a grave.

"Look at this. It's the eagle, the sign of Prince Andor." Arja's voice was hushed as she pointed to the gravestone.

"I wouldn't touch that if I were you," Finnar said. "The dragon's determined to protect the princess. If you desecrate Prince Andor's grave, she'll probably get upset and send the dragon after you."

"I was just trying to see it better," Arja shot back. "I can't see the runes on it, so I wanted to move it so I could read it better. I wasn't going to 'desecrate' it."

The grass behind them shifted, and Pyri appeared behind them. "I'm sure your brother only means well, Lady Arja."

Arja bit her lip, keeping her temper in check as Finnar smiled.

Pyri sighed and looked forward. "It does help his point that grave is cursed land."

"Eydis is cursed, itself," Arja reminded her. "Why is this place different?"

"Because it's my father's grave."

Arja took a step back. Beside her, Finnar's mouth dropped open as he looked from the tower to the dirt mound, and then from the grave stone to Pyri.

"You're Prince Andor's daughter?" Arja asked. "But that means that … "

She looked over at the castle and then back at the older woman before her. Her hand went down to her waist, where she realized she'd forgotten her sword back in the room. Finnar came to the same conclusion, but Pyri only chuckled.

"There is no reason to fear me," Pyri assured them. "My mother has never been happy with my refusal to support her, but I am still hers—at least, enough so that she didn't kill me, like she did my father."

Arja looked back at the grave. "I thought some rebellious bandits were the ones who killed him."

Pyri nodded. "That is true, actually, but they weren't so much rebellious bandits as they were fierce loyalists to my mother. My father is thought to be quite the noble man, but that is not the truth."

"Another legend," Arja murmured, thinking of Bjorn's earlier assessment that legends were full of lies.

"I was quite upset when I found out the truth," Pyri said. "My mother was pregnant with me when she found out about my father's wandering heart. I wouldn't be surprised if I have several brothers and sisters in Oseberg and even in Kyvan."

"That's terrible," Arja said. She took hold of Finnar's arm, more grateful than ever that she had grown up in a loving home, even if it felt crowded at times.

"It was." Pyri stared forward, her eyes glazing over with memories. "I never knew my father personally. But I never agreed with my mother, that he deserved to die as he did. The bandits captured him, and rather than kill him right away, they prepared him for a blood eagle death."

Arja felt sick; the blood eagle was the cruelest form of punishment and reserved for the most vile traitors. The man decreed to die would have an eagle carved into his back before his spine was sliced open and cut from his ribs. As he died, his ribs would be pulled from his body to make wings, which would then be covered with his lungs.

"So many people think it's because he was such a noble man, but it's not true," Pyri said. "Those of us who know the truth—those who live here on the island and participated in the prince's death—enjoy the irony of his reputation."

Arja reached over and patted Pyri's arm. "I'm so sorry."

She shook her head. "My mother was quite the sheltered child growing up. Her father arranged a marriage, and she was pleased when he picked Prince Andor. My father was handsome, I am told."

There's more to love than beauty. Arja thought back to Ana's adamant retort. How long had she been around the princess to learn such a painful truth so well?

"When my mother discovered his indiscretions, she was already pregnant with me," Pyri said. "Her father had recently died, and so she had nothing but me. And in her grief, she was torn apart."

"That's why the dragon came," Arja said, unable to stop a tear from slipping from her eye. "It was because the princess was in pain. The dragon wanted to punish the men who came looking for beauty and power."

"That's why it's a girl, too," Finnar said. His voice was soft, but Arja still turned around to glare at him. He shrugged, and Arja decided to reserve her ire as he added, "I meant that she wouldn't likely trust a male dragon at the time, especially if her father was dead and her husband had just betrayed her."

"I imagine so," Pyri agreed in a light tone. "All these years since, I've watched over my father's grave to remind myself of my mother's capacity for evil. It's easy to forget, as terrible as it sounds. As much as I admired my mother when I was younger, I've seen her enchant countless men and lure them here to fight her dragon."

"Is that why you don't have a tattoo?" Arja asked. "You don't agree with her?"

Pyri nodded. "As I said, I am protected from her wrath, since I share her blood, and there's enough humanity inside of her that she won't go against me. I began growing flowers when I was younger, and my mother encouraged me. It even allowed some of her goodness to come back, and we were able to bound over it. You may have noticed that Ana and I get along quite well."

Arja frowned, not sure what Ana had to do with anything.

"I like to think my life would have been very different, had my father honored his wedding vows." Pyri gestured toward the rolling hills and fields of flowers behind her. "So many lives have been damaged because of my father, but my mother has only made it worse."

"Including ours," Finnar said glumly.

"Including yours," Pyri agreed. "These flowers are beautiful, but they can't make up for all the blood that's been shed and sacrificed over the last century."

Arja thought of the own methods she'd to get Finnar and Bjorn to Eydis; her head fell into her hands.

Every drop of deceit she'd carried since fending off Sterlig's insufferable marriage proposal leaked into her mind. She saw herself taunting him, telling him he was hardly brave, and all the reports of his deeds were nothing if he couldn't take down the dragon of Eydis, especially if it was for her hand. Arja remembered the shock and disbelief, and then the fear when she learned her brothers had left with him; and then she thought of all the pressure she put on Bjorn after Sterlig's departure. She had only wanted Bjorn to admit he wanted her, so she would be safe if Sterlig did manage, somehow, to defeat the dragon. And then, after they heard the news and the nightmares came, Arja remembered her latest performance in Bjorn's forge, as she offered herself to him in marriage for the sake of convenience rather than anything she felt or believed.

And after she'd finally admitted to all of this to Bjorn—after he gave her his mother's cross and the love he had in his own heart for her—he'd walked away.

And rightfully so.

"Is that Bjorn?"

Pyri's question made Arja look up again. She followed Pyri's gaze further into the heart of the island, where the moonflower fields blossomed in abundance.

There, in the center of their white buds, was Bjorn.

Arja closed her eyes briefly, her hand covering the crucifix under her tunic. "Thank the Allfather. It's Bjorn."

"Something is wrong," Pyri said. There was a wildness to her milky irises. She gasped a moment later, and Arja could see what frightened her.

A single sliver of brilliant white stood tall behind Bjorn, as a bolt of lightning lit up the sky in the distance.

Princess Brynja was there, and she was clearly calling for her dragon.

Arja saw Bjorn was standing there in his leather hide pants and a woolen tunic; even from where she was standing, Arja could see his sword was at his side, and it was glowing as it hung on his belt. But Bjorn didn't seem to notice what was happening.

Finnar's eyes went wide, and his mouth dropped open. "By the gods," he choked out.

Arja looked back at Pyri. "Is he in danger?"

"If he left my house without any protection, he is."

The dragon roared as thunder crackled.

Finnar looked around nervously. "We'd better go get him."

"It might be too late," Pyri told him, pointing to the skies. There was a large shadow rising from behind the clouds.

Arja felt her heart sink.

Bjorn was in trouble.

And it was all her fault.

❖　　❖　　❖

Bjorn barely noticed the coming storm clouds as he stared at Princess Brynja.

When he'd left Pyri's house, he had intended to go and find Camille, or see if he could find a forge on the island. He longed for the security that work offered him. The days of dealing with Arja—and the clashing, emotional storm between them—had finally been too much for him. He had given her his heart, and it turned out she had betrayed his brother and lied to him.

Working with iron proved to be much less troublesome. And when, seemingly suddenly, he had found himself in the middle of a field of moonflowers, he had a feeling his troubles were only going to get worse.

His premonition was confirmed when Princess Brynja appeared beside him. He gaped at her, watching as she walked over the flowers to stand before him.

She wore a long white dress, one that was cut with simple lines and long fabrics; it added a graceful air to her walk as her skirts trailed through the grass behind her. Princess Brynja had the air of vulnerability around her, and Bjorn couldn't stop himself from softening in sympathy. Her eyes were a startling gray, while her hair was just as white as her dress. She almost looked like a young version of Pyri.

The princess stood in front of him and offered him a sad smile.

Feeling awkward, Bjorn gave her quick bow. He remained silent, unsure of what to say, and Brynja seemed to approve.

"What do you think of my flowers, Bjorn of Kyvan?"

Bjorn felt his breath catch in his throat. Brynja's voice was husky and mellow, a strange combination of music that demanded his attention. He cleared his throat, careful not to show his concern.

Where is Arja when I need her?

Bjorn quickly put that thought aside as Princess Brynja reached down and picked one of her moonflowers. The bloom opened up as she held it, and the scent caught on the air.

"They're lovely, aren't they?" Brynja asked.

"Yes." Bjorn swallowed hard and focused on the rows of vines where Eydis' famous blooms were slowly opening as the misty sunlight fell away from them. It was then he noticed the storm coming over the horizon.

"You don't need to worry about the weather," Brynja told him. "The extra rain is good for my blossoms."

"I didn't think you ever left your tower." Bjorn glanced back at the castle, still half-hidden in the mountain. He felt his palms start to sweat. "Have you come here to check on them?"

"I leave my tower from time to time, but only for special instances," Brynja said. "When I saw you out here, I wanted to make sure you weren't hurting my crop."

"Oh, no." Bjorn shook his head. "I know the people of Kyvan enjoy the perfume from Eydis."

He glanced around again, trying to show her he had been careful not to trod on the flowers. But as he looked, Bjorn grew increasingly uncomfortable.

He didn't remember walking this way after leaving Pyri's house, and there were no clear footprints behind him.

"You've never bought the perfume yourself, have you?" Brynja asked.

This was no place for a conversation, Bjorn thought, suddenly eager to leave.

But what choice did he have? He took a step back, and Brynja took a step forward.

Seeing no other recourse, Bjorn shook his head. "No, but I know of those who do, and I know the depth of their love for each other."

He thought of Arja's parents, and how often he'd seen Arja talk with Camille before while she was trading in Kyvan.

"Why not?" Brynja asked, taking another step closer to him. He stepped back again, but he stumbled as he came into contact with someone else.

He jerked around to see a little girl, watching him carefully with her honey-colored eyes.

"Watch it," she said. "I'm playing here."

He quickly apologized, and Brynja giggled.

"You'll have to excuse Ana," the princess said, watching Ana as she ran off and began to dance in the fields. "She loves to play in the flowers. When I saw you come this way, I knew she would enjoy it, too."

THE LEGEND OF EYDIS

"I see." Bjorn put his hand back on his sword, and that was when he felt the scalding heat radiating from his sword. He loosened his grip as he noticed the sword was glowing its angry green again.

Sterlig.

Bjorn looked from the sword to Ana. Sterlig had never been around children, even though he'd professed he would have an abundance of them.

Could it be Ana? Or is it the princess?

Bjorn's thoughts were interrupted as Brynja sighed. Her sadness resonated with his own.

"Are you well, Princess?" he asked.

"How can I be well, with this broken heart of mine?" Brynja asked.

Broken heart.

Bjorn gripped his sword's pommel more tightly as he remembered his own runic inscription on his blade.

"Tell me, Bjorn of Kyvan, you are obviously a man of honor. Do you think you can love me?" Brynja asked, her full lips frowning into a perfect pout.

"No."

His answer was unintentionally brusque, and as he watched Brynja's gray eyes widen, Bjorn knew he might have laughed, if it had been Arja. From the shock of her expression, he doubted anyone had ever told Brynja no before, especially when it came to loving her.

"I mean no disrespect, Princess, and I apologize if it seemed that way." He gave her a bow of respect. "But my answer is no."

"I will forgive you for that, but I must ask how you believe yourself to be so certain?" Brynja walked up beside him and took his arm, resting her soft cheek against his shoulder.

Bjorn tried to dislodge himself from her grip, but it was surprisingly firm. As gently as he could, he pulled his arm out from hers and took another step back.

"I must honor you and speak the truth," he said, starting to feel crowded as she advanced on him. "And the truth is, I've already lost my heart to another, and I can't imagine a world without her."

No matter how difficult she makes everything else.

As welcome as the thought of Arja was, it also pained him. If she was here, she would chastise him for his inability to handle women and their softer affections properly.

"Have you always told the truth to those you've loved?" There was a more pointed quality to Brynja's voice now; her voice was no longer so melodious.

"No." Bjorn thought of Arja and their earlier fight. He shook his head. "How else would I know the cost of a lie so well?"

"The one who was supposed to love you could have been lying, as well," Brynja said. "Those who lie know the cost, but the people lied to know it, too."

"That is part of life, I'm afraid," Bjorn said quietly. "A very central one, too—that men are fallen beings, living in a fallen world."

Brynja narrowed her eyes. "I see."

Her voice had hardened into a hiss, and he felt another pang of regret for his careless answer. Bjorn hated to think she actually did like him and hope he would be the one to slay the dragon for her.

"I am sorry if others' lies have hurt you," Bjorn said quietly. "I will not add to your grief in that regard. I can't be in love with you, and from what I know of you, Princess, of all people, you would understand my feelings for the woman I love. Prince Andor was your true love, and you wouldn't want to just replace him with another, no matter how useful or beneficial it was to do so, would you?"

Bjorn turned around, looking for Pyri's house again. Mist was flying in from the surrounding sea, but he thought he could make out the shape of Pyri's house in the distance.

"A princess is bound to do what she believes is best for her people, no matter who she loves," Brynja said.

"Just as a man is bound by his honor to do what he can for those he loves." He had come to Eydis for that very reason, after all. He had come with Arja in hopes of getting her peace over Sterlig's death. Now, he also knew that to avenge his brother, he had come to slay the princess' dragon, and in doing so, he would free the princess and the people bound by its blood.

Brynja eyed him, looking reluctantly amused. "You seem determined to slay the dragon of Eydis, even though you have admitted you cannot love me. It's been a hundred years, but this is the first time this has happened."

"Is that really so surprising?" Bjorn asked, caught off guard by her surprise.

Her lips thinned into a bitter smile. "After a hundred years, I have been disappointed quite a few times, Bjorn of Kyvan."

He could hear the pain in her voice.

Bjorn looked away from her. He saw the small girl, Ana, as she continued to play in the flowers. She was a beautiful little girl, and it was fun to watch her frolic, picking flowers, pulling their petals off, and rolling in the fields. She was free and innocent in a way that only a child could ever be.

There was something else about her, too, and Bjorn wasn't sure what it was exactly.

Perhaps Ana made him think of his own children, the ones he could possibly have with

Arja—if they could find a way to love each other together, and if Arja changed her mind about children.

He frowned. No. That was not the reason Ana caught his attention.

"If you are not here out of love for me, then can I assume you are here for the material rewards?" Brynja asked, touching his cheek affectionately. "You would slay the dragon and free my people, and you would be declared king of this island."

"No," Bjorn answered, reaching for his sword. "It's a matter of honor for my brother, as little as he apparently deserves it."

In the fields, Ana suddenly stopped playing. She stood there, her body standing tall and rigid. Not even her hair stirred against the wind.

That was when Bjorn realized why Ana seemed strange.

There are no other children here on Eydis.

"Who is Ana?" Bjorn asked. "Is she your daughter?"

Brynja surprised him by laughing. "Why so curious? Would you like to help me fill the island with more children, Bjorn? Whatever your heart tells you, your blood might yet change your mind about me. A man such as you, so talented and clearly underappreciated, surely should be one worthy of this island's kingship."

Brynja looped her arms through his again, her large, gray eyes looking up at him longingly. "It's not like the woman you love would give you so many if she had the chance, would she?"

Bjorn stepped away from the princess. He patted her hand patiently as he slipped free of her grasp, but he was more eager than ever to escape her.

"No, thank you, Your Highness. If you would, please excuse me."

He stepped back from her, slowly at first, and then more quickly as he saw the lovely innocence of her expression transform into righteous fury.

"Kiss me," she hissed, lunging after him. "I need you to kiss me, and I shall be free of the dragon's protection, Bjorn."

"What?" He scrambled back, desperate to get away from her.

"Only true love can defeat the dragon's power," Brynja said, her eyes starting to glow with scarlet. "Love will cast out all fear, and hate will lose all its power. And then the island will be free. All your new friends, and your brother, too—all of them will be free, if you only kiss me, Bjorn."

Bjorn shook his head. "I don't love you," he said. "I love—"

Before he could say anything else, he bumped into Ana, who was behind him. Jostled by the abrupt contact, Bjorn fell to one knee, and Brynja grabbed him.

THE LEGEND OF EYDIS

She leaned down just as he looked up, and her lips pressed against his in an awkward kiss.

Lightning clashed overhead, the seas tumbled, and a roar cried out from under the mountains. All of it was muted around Bjorn, as he smelled the sweet potency of the moonflowers surrounding them. Their hypnotizing scent burned into him, and before he could stop her, Brynja pressed her lips further down onto his.

Bjorn stilled briefly, struck by the power behind Brynja's kiss, but he quickly began struggling to back away from her as she cradled his face, her soft hands contrasting with the sharpness of her fingernails as they dug into his flesh.

And then he heard Arja calling out to him.

THE LEGEND OF EYDIS

16

          ❖   ❖   ❖

"Bjorn!"

Arja ran as fast as she could, desperate to reach Bjorn, calling for him in between deep breaths. She was getting closer, but she was still too far away. She could just see him as the coming rain sprinkled its first drops down through the growing mists. He was standing with Princess Brynja, and as she watched, Arja felt sick with overwhelming fear.

As Bjorn knelt, she stumbled. As she struggled to regain her balance, she watched in horror as the princess leaned down and kissed him.

No.

She stopped running, stricken at the sight. Arja felt her eyes sting with tears as her heart broke.

No matter what I've done to him, Bjorn wouldn't do this to me ... would he?

She had no claim on Bjorn—not when she'd deceived him and hidden as much as she had from him. The only thing she had of his was his mother's necklace, and he'd given it to her before she told him the truth. She covered her face with her hands, as if to hold back the flood of her inner grief.

Through her fingers, a flicker of red and green caught her eye.

Arja blinked away her tears and saw the sword at Bjorn's side. It was glowing with a fierce and furious green aura—one that clashed heavily with the red aura kindling around Brynja's body.

… All the red auras she'd seen from Camille's tattoo, and Finnar and Jon's eyes …

It's the dragon's power. The princess is using the dragon's power to bewitch Bjorn.

"Bjorn!" Arja cried out his name again in desperation.

Behind her, the winds barreled in from the sea, sending the flower petals dancing into the storm.

"Arja," Bjorn gasped as he twisted away from Brynja.

His sudden movement forced Brynja forward, and she fell to the ground, weeping. Her cries were as lovely as they were tragic, but Arja remained focused on Bjorn.

"Arja." Bjorn called her name, and then he came running for her.

Arja ran to meet him.

Her body crashed into his, her hope resurrected and her heart bursting with relief as she reached him. Her hands took hold of his face as he embraced her, and she buried her face in the crook of his shoulder.

And then a moment later, she was shaking him and yelling at him, anger over his disappearance overtook her sadness. "Bjorn! What were you thinking, leaving Pyri's house?"

"I wasn't," Bjorn replied. There was a somber look on his face as he tried to calm her down. "I didn't mean to go—"

"By the gods, I was so worried—"

"Arja." Bjorn took hold of her wrists and stopped her spirited assault. "I'm sorry."

"No, *I'm* the one who's sorry." Her voice nearly broke. She flung her arms around him again, fumbling to apologize properly. "You don't have anything to be sorry about."

Bjorn embraced her, and Arja buried her face into his chest, fighting off the urge to cry again.

"I thought I'd lost you," she whispered.

"I suppose that means it's really my fault, then? Since you belong to me?"

She let out a shaky laugh. His question was an answer more than anything else. She'd been so worried the princess would bewitch him, but he still belonged her. The rain sprinkled down on them as she leaned back to kiss Bjorn.

And then Ana screamed.

"Ana?" Bjorn loosened his hold on Arja as he looked around. "Where did she go? She was here a moment ago."

"She was here?" Arja glanced around. "I didn't see her. But then, I was only coming for you."

He gave her a tender smile. "Were you afraid I was in trouble because of our fight?"

"Bjorn, I—oh, no." Arja went silent as she finally saw the small lines of blood trickling down his cheeks. She raised her hand up to inspect his wound when Bjorn suddenly swept her off her feet.

"Watch out," Bjorn cried.

He twisted off to the side, pushing Arja out of the way as the dragon swept past, barely missing them as it flew toward the princess.

"Come to me, my dragon!" Brynja cried out, rivalling the roar of the dragon who landed behind her. She licked Bjorn's blood off her fingers as Bjorn and Arja stared at the mythic beast.

Arja's eyes widened at the sight of the sharp, scaly wings and the dark green skin of its underbelly from her nightmares. It reached into the sky, as tall as Brynja's castle tower, and its eyes were a demonic red that made her want to scream.

"Andorra, you're here at last," Brynja hissed, her own voice filling with venom.

Andorra. The dragon who had come to avenge Brynja and kill the treacherous men who would seek to use her for their own ends.

Brynja pet the nose of the dragon fondly. "You're a bit late today. But then, you've always enjoyed playing with your food before you eat it, haven't you?"

THE LEGEND OF EYDIS

In the blink of an eye, the calm and beautiful princess Arja had seen kiss Bjorn disappeared, as Brynja transformed into a Valkyrie of death. Her eyes blazed, her teeth sharpened, and all the flowers in her hair withered into stringy, black vines.

"Bjorn." Arja took hold of Bjorn's arm and tugged him back. "We must run for it. Finnar and Pyri went back to the house after we saw you. They're getting our weapons."

The dragon roared again, and the clouds broke open like floodgates. The raindrops turned into spikes, while the lightning fenced the island with its bolts.

"Andorra, attack them!"

The large dragon reared up on her hind legs, her wings outspread, nearly hiding the sky above them

Bjorn hurriedly shoved Arja away from its shadow. "Go, Arja!"

Arja stood her ground. "Bjorn—"

"Don't argue with me. I have to protect you." Bjorn unsheathed his sword.

"Bjorn." Arja gasped. "Look!"

The glowing sword shone with a green light, but the runic words inscribed into the blade glowed red.

Just like Brynja.

Arja turned to face the princess, just as the dragon took off.

"Move, Arja," Bjorn insisted, shifting his feet as he prepared to meet the dragon in battle.

THE LEGEND OF EYDIS

"But—"

Arja was cut off as she heard her name being called out from a distance.

"Arja!"

Finnar was approaching. Through the veil of rain and mist, Arja could just barely see him as he raced toward her. He carried her shield and sword as well as his own, and Pyri followed. The rain stopped around her, as if a small barrier of protection surrounded her frail body.

Arja's initial relief at having her weapons and being able to stand side-by-side with Bjorn against Brynja faded when Finnar slowed down. Panic writhed inside her: memories of Finnar trying to drown himself flashed through her mind. He stopped and fell to his knees. Arja could see he was staring intently at a spot behind her, and Arja didn't have to look to know he was watching Brynja. His eyes began to glow with a red fire, and he opened his mouth to scream.

"No." Arja's stomach turned as she saw him collapse. "Finn!"

Behind her, the dragon roared as it dived, and Bjorn raced forward, his sword held high. Arja stopped, torn between her brother and her beloved, as one faced down a dragon and one began to succumb to a demon.

"Arja, go," Bjorn shouted. Arja watched as he struck the dragon on its wing as it flew past him, but

THE LEGEND OF EYDIS

his blow did nothing to slow the mighty beast. "I'll be all right."

"No." She clenched her fists, desperate to save her brother, but she was torn at the thought of losing Bjorn.

"Just go," Bjorn insisted. "Go!"

Arja felt sick as she left Bjorn, but she saw no choice as she hurried forward. She ran to where Finnar was writhing in pain on the soaking wet ground, tangling himself in the frayed vines and crushed flowers.

She was almost to him when she tripped over another leg and fell, face-forward, into a small puddle of mud.

"Gross." Arja wiped her face off, pushing back her wet hair. She cleared her eyes to see Ana standing over her, looking down at her curiously.

"You're a bad lady, aren't you?" Ana's voice was a lot sharper than Arja remembered it.

"What are you doing here?" Arja asked.

"You are one of those bad ladies, who lies to men, aren't you?"

Arja felt her face burn with shame, before she remembered Ana worked for Brynja. There was no need for her to answer to the little girl.

"You're a bit young, Ana. And we're in trouble, so let's move. I need to help my brother."

Arja staggered to her feet, ignoring Ana's frown as she reached Finnar.

"Finn?" Arja tentatively put her hand on his shoulder. He bucked at her touch, grumbling nonsensical words and foaming at the mouth.

"What's happening?" Arja cried in frustration. "Finn!"

Ana appeared behind her again. "You can't help him."

"What do you mean?" Arja glared over at her, as she tried to get Finnar to sit up.

"He's under the dragon's power." Ana smirked. "He won't be better until the dragon is defeated, but no one's ever beaten Andorra."

The rain dissipated as Pyri came up beside them. "No one has won against Andorra, but there are those who have hurt the princess. Isn't that right, Ana?"

Arja glanced at the little girl, who had a sudden, frightened look on her face.

"We don't talk about that, Lady Pyri," Ana whispered.

"Of course not. You wouldn't be able to face the truth, would you?"

"Why are you doing this to me?" Ana yelled.

"It's time to say goodbye, Ana," Pyri said. "We have been friends a long time, and I will remember you always. But you need to go home now."

Arja saw Finnar relax as Pyri and Ana talked. Pyri's protective aura was still working, she realized. The princess's power wasn't able to work on Pyri. Finnar gradually blinked and his eyes faded back to blue.

"Daddy will protect me!" Ana shouted as she put her hands over her ears.

"He always loved you, but no parent can protect his child forever." Pyri's voice was loud, but she held out her hands in a gesture of apology. "And it is dangerous for Princess Brynja to pretend otherwise."

"I can pretend for as long as I want!" Ana insisted.

Pyri and Ana argued back and forth. From the way Ana talked, it was almost as if she was Brynja's sister.

But as the little girl stomped her foot into the mud again, Arja saw Ana still didn't leave any imprint on the ground.

"You're a ghost," Arja whispered, shocked.

Ana crossed her arms and stuck her tongue out at Arja. "I'm still real."

"She's the ghost of my mother's innocence," Pyri explained. "And if you are real, Ana, you have to come to terms with real things, too. That means accepting your father didn't protect you from Prince Andor's betrayal—"

"Stop it!" Ana yelled, covering her ears with her hands again.

"And realizing that even though he loved you, he was still human, and being human, he had to die," Pyri said. "You also have to realize that killing all the men who come here is wrong, just as it was wrong for my father to dishonor you the way he did."

"No!" Ana screamed again, this time much more loudly.

"Arja?" Finnar whispered.

"Finn," Arja cheered, trying to help him sit up. "You're all right."

Pyri turned to face them, as Ana continued to have her tirade. "You'll need to leave him here, Arja. I can protect him and keep Ana busy while you go and fight my mother and her dragon."

Arja stood up. "Even if it means we have to kill her?"

"Camille told you the truth already, didn't he?" Pyri gave her a sad smile. "She is already dead."

"I'm sorry." Arja looked away.

"Go," Pyri urged her. "You can't do anything here, but you can make a difference over there. With your beloved husband."

Arja grimaced. "He's not really my husband," she whispered, finally admitting the truth. She hated to admit her failing now, but when Pyri only smiled, she blushed.

"Isn't he, though?" Pyri pointed to her heart, where the crucifix from Bjorn's mother lovingly bumped against her breastbone. "He's pledged his heart to you and offered you a token of his love to show others as proof, has he not?"

Arja was about to tell her that there was no talk of the future, and that was not a certainty. But then the dragon roared again, and Arja heard Bjorn cry out in pain.

"Bjorn."

"Arja." Finnar nudged her and pointed to the items he'd dropped behind Pyri. "I got your shield."

"Thank you, Finn."

He gave her a tense nod, and she hurriedly grabbed her sword and shield, said a quick thanks to her brother, and hurried off, leaving the others behind as she raced to join Bjorn.

She was armed and ready to fight beside him in battle, and this time, she would not let him down.

❖ ❖ ❖

Bjorn gritted his teeth together and prepared to face down the dragon's charge, trying to catch his breath. Andorra hardly seemed to exert herself at all, and he had a feeling she was just toying with him.

"Think, think," he muttered to himself, struggling not to give into despair as doubts and fear plagued him.

259

What did he really know about fighting? He could almost hear Sterlig chiding him for using his time to work with Lodd instead of training.

Bjorn had used his talent to create the weapon, but that was not enough to win, was it?

Even Sterlig had used his sword and failed.

He glanced down at it, surprised to see it was not glowing as fiercely as it had before, when he'd been caught under Brynja's power.

Something tugged at his memory, and he looked back at the dragon.

The great beast was every bit as big and terrifying as he'd seen in his dreams. Sterlig's fear before his death suffocated Bjorn's mind as much as it sharpened it.

Andorra reared up onto her hind legs, flapping her wings viciously as she prepared to take flight once more.

Bjorn wiped the rainwater from his face and held his sword ready.

But that was when he noticed Brynja was no longer a spectator. She was retreating, heading through the wet fields, heading back toward her castle as it continued to rain.

"Bjorn." Arja's voice was soft behind him. He turned to see her, and face an even bigger fear.

I can't lose her now.

"Arja, please. I don't want you here," Bjorn said. "I said I would protect you. Go get Finnar and Ana out of here. Take them to Pyri's house."

"Pyri's taking care of them," Arja said as she stood firm beside him. "I was in her way. And anyway, you promised me that we would work together when we got to Eydis."

"This isn't exactly what I had planned," Bjorn shouted, as the dragon roared again. He raced forward, preparing another attack.

"I thought we didn't have a plan," Arja shouted back, racing behind him.

Bjorn groaned at her attempt at humor, but before he could chastise her, the dragon soared at them.

He raised his sword and cut downward, aiming for a spot on the dragon's underbelly. His blade sliced into the larger stomach area, and he nearly dropped it at the ferocity of the impact. Beside him, Arja slashed at the dragon's tail.

"See?" Arja huffed through deep breaths. "We're better when we work together."

He gave her a quick smile, and then pointed to the ground. "I think the dragon's bleeding."

There was a lot of mud from the rain, but there was one single, thick streak of brownish red that lined the ground. Several rusty specks dotted the moonflowers that were still blooming.

"I felt my blow land," Arja said.

Bjorn nodded. "We need to hit it in the same spot again. If we can injure it, we might be able to defeat it."

He dared not hope for such an outcome. Surely there had to be more to defeating a dragon. After all, Sterlig had learned how to hunt and kill wild animals from their father, same as Bjorn. Even if Sterlig didn't have a plan when he arrived on Eydis, surely even he would've been able to figure that out.

Had Brynja's beauty and presence bewitched Sterlig enough that he would forget about that? Bjorn frowned. He hadn't always gotten along with his brother, and he felt more guilty than sad at his death—but he also knew his brother's abilities, and Sterlig had been an excellent hunter.

"We can do it," Arja said. "I am shieldmaiden of Kyvan, after all."

"All right. Be careful. And follow after me. I'll take the brunt of the attack."

"But—"

"Don't argue with me," Bjorn shouted back. "I have to be seen protecting my wife, don't I?"

"Oh, Bjorn." She rolled her eyes, but he felt vindicated when she stepped back to cover him. Her sword was held at the ready as the dragon circled around the castle tower.

It seems smaller now. Bjorn frowned, but a moment later, he saw it was true. The cut from its underbelly was leaking, and the dragon was shrinking in size as it lost its blood.

Bjorn narrowed his eyes. He'd grown up hearing the legend of Eydis his whole life. He'd read of monsters like the Nephilim and the leviathan, and he'd heard tales of Odin and Loki and Hel, and the other gods of Snæland.

He glanced over at Arja. A glimmer of gold flickered at her neck.

She was wearing his mother's crucifix, and his memory stirred. His mother dismissed the gods of his nation as demons in disguise, and even demons were subjected to the power of God the Allfather. He prayed she was right as the dragon roared again.

"Arja?" he called back.

"What is it, now?"

"I love you."

She held her position, but Bjorn saw her fingers tighten around her sword's hilt. "Does that mean you can forgive me for all of this?"

Bjorn knew Arja was always used to taking care of others and helping them, and when she was able to be on her own, she hated relying on others. Even now, she was willing to risk her life to be with him during this battle, and she was more concerned with being forgiven than being protected. She might have seen her question as a sign of weakness, but Bjorn welcomed it. If they were going to be together, they would have to learn to grow together.

"Yes." He watched as her eyes lit up with solemn hope. "And if we survive, you can spend the rest of your life making it up to me."

"I love you, Bjorn," Arja whispered. She slid closer to him, her sword still held up high as mud gathered under their feet, and the scent of the dying flowers wafted up in the rain. "And just so you know, you don't have to slay the dragon for me."

"No. We have to slay the dragon for Sterlig, and for the others on the *Sea Serpent*," Bjorn said, nodding toward the docks, where the ships were all getting pummeled with rain. He saw Arja smile at him with pride. "And for the princess, too."

Arja lost her smile. "I don't particularly care about her."

"She's as much a prisoner of this island as they are."

The dragon left off circling the tower and began to fly towards them.

"She's the princess, Bjorn." Arja held up her sword again. "She might be a prisoner, but she still has plenty of power here. She's the one who killed Prince Andor."

"She killed him?" Bjorn frowned. "That's not in the legend."

"I'm sure they didn't want to proclaim she had him killed by blood eagle. It would deter a lot of sympathy," Arja said. "Finn found his grave behind Pyri's house."

Blood eagle.

Prince Andor had been a sacrifice.

"Arja, we need to get to the princess." He ground his feet more firmly into the ground, preparing his attack as he put his plan together.

"What? Why?"

Before Bjorn could explain, the dragon attacked.

The beast roared and dived at them. Bjorn clipped the dragon's neck, while Arja managed to cut down the length of a wing.

They battled the dragon, stabbing their swords at the beast, feinting attacks, and covering for each other. The dragon pushed back, whipping its tail and slamming into them at every turn.

Arja whimpered when a claw caught her shoulder, and Bjorn's chest tightened in fear. "Are you all right?"

The dragon took off skyward again, slipping into the clouds, and Bjorn followed it with his gaze as he hurried over next to her, his muscles aching.

"I'll be fine," Arja said, but he saw her shield drop.

As the dragon looped around and again flew toward them, a glimmer of white at the top of the tower caught Bjorn's eye.

There, standing on the balcony, Brynja was watching them, her eyes full of blood and laughter.

The next second, he ducked as Andorra's claws swiped at him, though he landed a cut on her wing.

THE LEGEND OF EYDIS

The dragon roared, but what caught Bjorn's attention was his blade. The glowing aura on his sword had changed. Earlier, the runic inscription had been bathed in an angry red, while the rest of the blade was green. Now it was all green.

It was all Bjorn needed to see; the last mystery was solved. He beckoned to Arja to follow him.

"Arja, hurry!" Bjorn breathed in hard as he jumped over the dragon's tail. "I know how to defeat the dragon."

"We are beating it," Arja pointed out. "Look."

She pointed to the dragon, who was bleeding from several wounds. It shrank in size, even as they watched.

"We might be winning now, but if we're going to slay it, we need the dragon's true blood." Bjorn looked back toward the castle tower. "And that means we need Princess Brynja."

17

As Bjorn headed toward the castle, Arja followed closely behind. Her body ached from fighting, and her bruises were sore. Her soaked tunic added more weight to her clothes, and she still had to worry about the dragon.

She glanced through the rain to see Brynja's beast was bleeding, with its multiple wounds dotted against its evergreen scales.

Bjorn had been smart to keep poking at its underbelly.

"There's the princess." Bjorn pointed to the balcony, before he pushed his wet hair out of his face.

Arja could see the little flash of white. "I guess she's back to being Brynja the Bride," she murmured, thinking of the princess' angelic moniker.

"Maybe we should call her the Bride of Death after this."

Arja felt weary, but she still managed a small chuckle. "I will agree to that."

The dragon roared behind them, screeching out in pain and fury.

"Here comes the dragon again. I'll take the lead." Bjorn ducked as the dragon flew close to the ground and charged at them.

Arja held her sword out, preparing to attack the dragon as it flew at her.

At the last moment, she swiveled to the side. "Got you," she yelled, as she stabbed the dragon in the eye.

The beast stopped flying and fell to its legs, roaring in furious pain. It snarled and bucked, spreading its wings out wide in chaotic agony. The ground was still slippery beneath her feet, but she dodged its swipes and landed another blow along its nostrils.

"Careful," Bjorn said, as he pulled Arja back toward the castle.

"It was a good attack, though," Arja said smugly. "You have to admit that."

"It was," Bjorn agreed. "But—"

The dragon suddenly appeared in front of them again, this time shrunk down to the size of a bear. Bjorn and Arja raced forward, eager to attack.

"Augh!" Bjorn rammed his sword through the belly again, causing the dragon to emit a whimpered cry.

Arja gritted her teeth. "Let's finish off this dragon, together."

"Yes." Bjorn nodded. "Together."

Arja gave him a small smile. The rain had weakened along with the dragon. Her shoulder was screaming in pain, and her feet ached from all her running. But as she looked at Bjorn, standing beside her, just as rain-soaked and disheveled, she only felt triumphant. His mother's cross bumped against her heart, and all the love she felt for him swelled up inside of her. Slaying the dragon of Eydis was nothing compared to the power she felt in surrendering her love to him, and gaining his heart in return.

"I love you," she whispered.

"I love you, too."

Together, they lunged forward.

Arja's sword struck hard through the dragon's underbelly as Bjorn's sword cut through its heart.

The dragon roared once more, and then it shrunk and fell away.

The body fell to the ground, twitching as their swords remained locked within its scaly flesh.

And when it was all over, the last of the dragon's blood pooled around it and turned black. As Arja watched, it sank into the earth and disappeared, the rain already washing the rest of it away.

"We did it."

Arja's voice was full of awe as the rain slowed to a drizzle, and the air tasted of flowers and sweat as she stared at the sight before her. "We did it, Bjorn."

"Not yet." Bjorn stepped forward and pulled his sword out of the blackened mud. "Look."

Arja was not sure of what he meant. But as she looked at the sword, she saw it was still glowing with a ghastly greenish tint.

Sterlig was still not able to rest in peace.

"The dragon's body might be defeated, but we still need its true blood. Princess Brynja conducted demonic sacrifice when she killed Prince Andor. That's how the dragon came to be; it was powerful, because of the man she killed, and how important he was to her."

Arja shivered. "That's awful."

"Demons use blood for power." Bjorn looked back at the castle tower, where Brynja still stood, waiting and watching over them. "And if we want to send it back to hell, that means we need to kill the host. Or we have to convince her to banish the demon herself."

"Can we do that?" Arja asked quietly.

Was there a way to save Princess Brynja without killing her?

He shrugged. "I don't know."

Arja heard footsteps approaching from behind them, and she felt strangely relieved when she heard Ana's voice.

THE LEGEND OF EYDIS

"Princess Brynja is ready to reward you for defeating the dragon of Eydis."

Arja and Bjorn exchanged a cautious look, and then he shrugged.

"We were going to go see her," Bjorn told Ana as he sheathed his sword. "Please, lead the way."

❁ ❁ ❁

As they walked behind Ana, Bjorn reached over and took Arja's hand. Her fingers laced around his, and he smiled.

He was tired and battered from their fight, but he was also energized with Arja by his side. Her shoulder was still bleeding some, but the injury was clean, thanks to the rain, and he knew it would heal in its own time. As Ana escorted them to the tower doors, he slowed his pace, allowing himself to embrace the chance to be with her in the aftermath of their victory—and to plan their next move.

As if she sensed his thoughts, Arja brushed up against him to whisper in his ear. "What's the plan, Bjorn?"

"I'm not sure," he admitted. "The dragon was not just any dragon; it was a monster she called to defend her island."

"And perhaps her heart, too," Arja said with a tired sadness in her voice. "Pyri told me and Finn that Brynja had killed Prince Andor because he was not faithful to her."

Bjorn gripped her hand in his. "You will never have to worry about that. I give you my oath on that, Arja."

"I know I can depend on you, Bjorn. You are an honorable man."

Seeing the blatant, adoring expression on her face, Bjorn would have given anything to lean over and kiss her. He resisted only because they had another battle ahead of them. But the months after Sterlig's death where they were apart seemed so long that slaying a dragon seemed easy by comparison.

All he had to do now was help his brother's spirit find peace, see if they could save Brynja, and get back home to Kyvan. Then they could embrace life together.

"We're here." Ana's voice was almost glum as the large doors to the castle opened before them.

Arja straightened, and Bjorn put his other hand on the hilt of his sword. Even in its sheath, he could still make out the blade's aura, which only grew brighter as Ana led them inside and up the long, winding stone staircase.

This is the right way. I know it.

At the top of the tower was a bedroom, furnished with items of luxury, from silken sheets to the ornately carved bedpost. There was a doorway opened onto the balcony, and a soft, sweet breeze was blowing in.

And there, in the middle of the room, as stately and beautiful as ever, was Brynja the Bride.

She was wearing her long white robes again, which, despite her earlier trek outside, were blisteringly white and pure. The flowers in her hair had blossomed again, and while Bjorn had promised Arja he would never fail her, he still felt her hand tighten around his.

He was grateful for her hesitation; he had his own concerns about why Brynja was suddenly much more angelic.

She smiled at them graciously. "You've done it, my noble warrior and my fearless shieldmaiden. You've destroyed the dragon of Eydis."

Brynja's smile only brightened as she stepped forward.

Bjorn took a step back, bumping into Ana. The little girl scowled up at him, her honey-colored eyes darkened to black.

"Sorry," he murmured, but her eyes only narrowed.

"You'll have to forgive Ana," Brynja said. "She is only concerned for me. She has been my companion and helper throughout the last century. I would not have been able to survive without her. Now, I must give the two of you your reward for slaying the dragon of Eydis."

"With all due respect, Princess Brynja," Bjorn said. "We cannot accept it. Not when the dragon is still alive."

"What do you mean?" she asked, laughing delicately. "Of course the dragon is dead."

"But it's not the dragon that is the real monster here on the island, is it, Princess?" Arja asked. She held up her sword and pointed it at Brynja's heart. "It still lives on inside of you."

"Oh, no," Brynja said. "I don't know what you're talking about. The dragon has always guarded me and the island, but now it is gone."

He knew of demons from some of his past readings. There were stories of old where demons had corrupted leaders and ordinary folk, and even animals, but as he came face to face with Princess Brynja, Bjorn suddenly wondered if she even knew the truth of her own possession.

She had to have allowed it to come in, especially after killing Prince Andor for his unfaithfulness.

At his side, the pommel of his sword grew hot. Bjorn reached for it, watching as Brynja's eyes narrowed. Her sky-gray irises suddenly sparkled scarlet, but she made no move against him.

"It is not gone," Bjorn said. "But I wonder if you can see it, Princess?"

He carefully let go of Arja. He saw her objection, and quickly shook his head. "Give me a moment."

"For what?" Arja asked, blistered. "We need to kill her, don't we?"

"I'm seeing if I can save her," Bjorn said quietly.

Arja huffed, but she nodded. "All right. Try."

Before he could do anything else, Ana began to cry. Arja and Bjorn both glanced back at her.

"Can't we just let them go?" Ana wailed. "Just let them leave, Princess. They're hurting me."

Bjorn turned back to Brynja. "Princess, please. I'm sorry Prince Andor hurt you. But perhaps it would be best to forgive him, so he can stop causing you this kind of pain—"

"Stop!" Ana wailed. She was shaking, putting her hands over her ears. "I don't want to hear this anymore! It hurts."

"But it's the truth," Arja said. She turned back to the princess. "And I know what that feels like. Sterlig came here and pledged himself to you after promising himself to me. And you didn't stop him, did you?"

"Sterlig Kyvansson was a fool," Ana said as she shook her head. "You are better off without him."

"Not everyone would say so," Arja said. She pulled on her necklace chain and brought out the cross Elska had given to Bjorn. "His mother wouldn't agree with that."

Ana went silent as she stared at the crucifix in Arja's palm. Her eyes went blank, and it was Brynja who began to moan.

"No … no," Brynja cried.

Bjorn and Arja both turned to watch in horror as Brynja's screams grew louder. She held her head and tore out her hair while her eyes burned with blood.

Her clothes transformed back, the white decomposing away into black. Her face began to decay, as the skin peeled away from her bones.

"I'm guilty of this," Ana whispered. "I'm guilty."

"What are you talking about?" Bjorn held up his sword as Brynja transformed. "Arja? Do you know?"

"Bjorn." Arja slid back from Ana, her eyes wide as she remembered what Pyri had said when she'd gone to help Finnar. "Pyri said Ana was the ghost of Brynja's innocence."

"How?" Bjorn asked.

Arja only shrugged, while Ana continued to wail.

"I did this. I did terrible things. Father will hate me for this!" Ana cried.

"Father is the one responsible for all of this," Brynja hissed at Ana. "If Father had only chosen a better man to marry me, I wouldn't be here like this!"

"I don't know," Arja gasped, as Bjorn pushed her back from Ana. They stood in a circle around the tower as Brynja spewed demonic auras, while Ana was slowly fading.

Brynja advanced on Ana, reaching out for her. "You were supposed to stay safe," she accused. "You didn't listen! And now Andorra must devour you, too."

Ana whimpered as Brynja reached for her.

"Stop it," Arja cried. "Ana's just a little girl."

"Hardly," Brynja grumbled. "She needs to grow up. Father never loved me, and neither did Prince Andor. Why would Father fail me? And why would Andor betray me?"

Ana screamed once more, her cry pure anguish as Brynja lunged forward, brandishing a dagger she'd had hidden at her side and plunged into the heart of the little girl.

Ana disappeared in one last bright, scorching light.

Arja and Bjorn covered their eyes, but when Ana's scream went silent, there was nothing more of her that remained—other than Brynja, who only smiled.

"You're the devil," Bjorn shouted.

"No, I'm not." Brynja's hollowed eyes burned with scarlet fire. "But I work for him. And so does Andorra."

Bjorn frowned, as he saw her eyes move to Arja.

A second later, Arja screamed in pain, as a small, slinky dragon suddenly jumped on her injured shoulder.

"Arja!" Bjorn cried out in shock, as the palm-sized dragon began to eat the flesh at Arja's shoulder. He watched as she grabbed a hold of it and tried to wrestle it free. Before he could move to help her, Brynja attacked.

She charged at Arja, wielding her dagger, and Bjorn didn't stop to think. He planted himself into her pathway and held his sword steady.

Brynja never faltered, even as Bjorn's sword stabbed right into her heart. Her dagger slipped harmlessly out of her hand at the impact.

Brynja screamed as the green aura of the sword burned through her. The red runic inscriptions lit up with blood and power, consuming Brynja in a blazing fire. Her clothes were eaten by the supernatural flames, before the fire encompassed her face. Andorra's tiny form disappeared into the heart of the fire.

When it became too hot to hold, Bjorn pushed his sword further into her heart, and then let it go.

He turned away, hiding his eyes from the brightness of Brynja's ghostly pyre as her scream resounded throughout the tower. He knelt in front of Arja to shield her until, at last, Brynja's cries disappeared.

Silence fell, and nothing seemed to be the same.

Cautiously, Bjorn stood up and reached a hand down to Arja.

"Bjorn." She clasped onto him tightly, still shaking. "What was that?"

"I don't want to think about it," Bjorn said as he cautiously stood up. He looked around. Ana was gone. Brynja was gone, and so was her dragon. Everything in the room, all the furniture, the chairs, the bed, and even the sheets all began to darken with age first, and then fiery shadows.

All that remained was his sword, which was laying on the stone floor before them.

As he watched, Bjorn saw the green glow, surrounding the red runic inscription.

"Bjorn, look." Arja pointed down at the sword as the aura began to move upward, molding itself into a familiar form.

"Sterlig." Bjorn's heart raced with uncertainty at the sight of his lost brother's ghost.

Sterlig said nothing as he looked at the two of them. His eyes were full of unspoken words, and Bjorn swallowed hard. He didn't know if he should say anything or if there was anything he could do.

And then Sterlig nodded, giving them a humbled bow, before his spirit faded away into nothing.

Bjorn and Arja both exchanged an uncertain look as the sword lost its glowing auras and the blade burned black.

Bjorn let out a slow breath.

It was over now.

<u>18</u>

❖   ❖   ❖

"Arja, you're bleeding."

Bjorn's voice cut through her muddled thoughts as she stared at the sword on the ground. It was blackened with fire and blood.

"Arja?"

"I'll be all right." Arja touched her shoulder tentatively, letting the small trickle of blood warm her fingers. She was still shaking, even her heart slowly started to return to its normal tempo.

She blinked as she saw Bjorn's tunic was slashed open, and he had several injuries. She frowned. "You're bleeding, too."

He gave her a quick grin. "I'll be all right."

"Oh, Bjorn." She rolled her eyes at his attempt at humor, before she leapt into his arms. Her heart was back to normal, but her head ached and she didn't know whether to laugh or cry, now that everything was over.

For a long moment, Bjorn held onto her, and Arja could feel his determination to keep her close. He was wet with rain and sweat and blood, but she felt the strength and power surround her and carry her, and she buried herself as far into him as she could.

THE LEGEND OF EYDIS

"It's all right now. The nightmares should be over," Bjorn whispered.

"Good." She stood up on her tiptoes to kiss him. "That means my dreams can come true."

She closed her eyes as he kissed her back. She could tell he was being careful not to hurt her as he held onto her. Her hands moved up his chest and she wrapped her arms around his neck.

A loud rumbling noise interrupted them.

"What was that?" Bjorn asked. He slowly let her go and headed toward the balcony as the ceiling cracked.

The two of them exchanged a worried glance.

"The tower's falling," Arja grabbed his arm and pulled him after her. "Bjorn, we have to get out of here."

Together, they fled from the room, not even bothering to retrieve any of their weapons. They hurried down the stairs as the tower started to collapse.

Bjorn and Arja burst through the tower doors as dust and stone fell down fast. The dust and debris billowed up into clouds and burst across the sky.

"Arja!"

Arja turned to see Finnar limping toward them, with Pyri walking slowly behind him.

"Finn," Arja cried happily, as she ran up and embraced him. "We did it, Finn. We did it!"

"I know." Her brother laughed and twirled Arja around in a celebratory circle. "I feel normal again for the first time in months."

"Oh, thank the Allfather," Arja cheered. "That means Jon is safe now, too!"

"I'm glad." Bjorn grinned. "It's time for all of us to move on from the past."

"I couldn't agree more." Finnar put Arja down and wrapped his arm around Bjorn's shoulders. "So this means you will finally marry my sister, then?"

"Finnar." Arja put her hands on her hips, giving her brother a disapproving look. "That's none of your business."

"After all this time, it should be." Finnar huffed. "Bjorn's not the type of man to just take the woman he wants."

"That's true," Bjorn said. "There is no taking you, Arja, if you don't take me, too."

Arja laughed. "If that's all it took, we would've been married months ago."

Before she could kiss Bjorn again, Finnar looped his other arm around Arja, embracing both of them. "Well, there it is. Welcome to the family, Bjorn!"

"I can only hope my family will be so delighted," Bjorn said.

"Your mother will be," Arja told him, cupping his cheek. "And your father won't be able to say anything. Since you're marrying me, my dowry can cancel out all his debts, and now that Sterlig's been avenged, Keyvak Ragnork can only sulk over your victory. And that makes him a truly spiteful, unhappy man."

"*Kona.*" Bjorn leaned into her palm and kissed it, before he picked her up.

Arja flushed at the endearment and held on tightly as Bjorn held her against him.

Finnar grinned. "Well, I have to put up with all your silly lover's smiles, but thank the gods this is over. All of it is over, and we can go home now."

"Yes, Finn," Bjorn said. "We can go home, and as your new brother, I can help you find a wife of your very own, too."

Finnar wrinkled his nose. "Go back to kissing Arja, would you?"

Another rumbling noise, much louder than the tower falling, rang out, making the smile fall from Finnar's face.

"What is it?" Bjorn asked, as the ground started to shake under his feet. "Is the mountain falling, too?"

Arja looked up to see rocks were rolling down the mountain behind where the castle once stood, but it wasn't the only one. The mountains were all falling over, while the ground was folding into itself.

"Bjorn! Arja!" Pyri called out to them as she hobbled over. She was holding up her skirts as she ran, looking more frail than ever. "Please, we must go."

"Lady Pyri, what's wrong?" Bjorn asked.

Arja nearly gasped to see Pyri. She was aging years at a time, right before their eyes.

"The curse is broken," Pyri explained. "Eydis no longer has a dragon to watch over the island, so it is sinking into the ocean. The seas will reclaim its wretchedness."

"The island is sinking," Finnar exclaimed. He took hold of Pyri's arm. "We better go."

Bjorn nodded and quickly took hold of Arja's hand. Together, the two of them helped Finnar and Pyri toward the docks. Bjorn saw that other island residents were tying their boats together to make room as the island sunk into the ocean. All of them seemed much more alive than before; many of them were not even frightened, and several seemed relieved to be leaving.

"Arja!" Camille waved his arm from the top deck of the *Sea Serpent* as they approached.

"Hold onto the ship for us," Arja called back.

Ephraim appeared behind Camille, his eyes narrowed. "We can't hold it forever! I want to get out of here and go home."

Bjorn and Finnar both guided Pyri onto the gangplank, while Arja took care to cast off the last of the ship's ropes.

Camille came down and took Pyri's hand reverently.

"Ah, my island princess," he said. "It is nice to be able to speak with you again."

Pyri smiled and nodded to the underside of his arm, which was now blank. "I see my mother's mark has been lost to time and circumstance."

"Unlike my affection for you, dear Pyri." Camille embraced her, and Finnar nudged Arja.

The island behind them continued to crumble. Arja held onto Bjorn as the island's mountains folded in, and the cove collapsed in on itself.

The sea swallowed the last of the island, leaving only the moonflower petals behind in the end.

As the island's location faded from sight, Arja saw other boats rowing up next to the *Sea Serpent*. They were full of other residents from Eydis, who were also rapidly aging as the curse faded.

"I guess it was a trick," Arja said. "If the dragon was slain, the one who defeated it would be proclaimed the ruler of a dead kingdom."

Bjorn pointed to the other boats. "We might need to help them."

"Look," Arja said, pointing up to Ephraim, who was calling out orders. "Ephraim's already trying to bring everyone together, so we can all arrive in Kyvan safely."

"They'll need more help than that."

"We'll be able to take care of it. After all, Camille and Ephraim are more receptive to our company this time," Arja murmured, and Bjorn smiled.

"I'm sure Ephraim is upset, and even more so if he's aged as much as Pyri has."

Pyri scoffed from behind him. "Age is but a number, Bjorn. I've been alive now for over a hundred years, along with everyone else on the island. I don't have much longer to live. But we still have time, and I believe it is best if I do so in Kyvan. I imagine I can make a few more years of a good living, so long as I have the last of my mother's gift."

Bjorn and Arja watched as Pyri pulled out a small bottle. Inside, Arja could see several wilted moonflowers and their seeds.

"Will your moonflowers grow on Snæland? Or were they only able to grow on Eydis because of the curse's power?" Bjorn asked.

"It might have a different scent when its finished," Pyri said. "But that is fine with me. I am only happy my mother can rest in peace now."

"Will you be able to make the perfume again?" Arja smiled up at Bjorn. "I think now that Bjorn has slain a dragon for me, he'll be in a good position to buy me some perfume."

Bjorn rolled his eyes, but Arja laughed.

"Perhaps. If I have some assistance." Pyri glanced over at Bjorn and then turned back to Arja with a sly look. "If you are not busy with your little ones by then."

Arja blushed. "I think we may need some time to recover from this adventure first," she said. She brightened. "Unless you are talking about Ulf? Perhaps he'll be ready to breed by next year."

"I think even that might need to wait." Bjorn laughed and kissed Arja on the forehead. "You are my next adventure, Arja, and I have a feeling this one will be even more legendary than the last."

Arja fell against him with a small laugh. "You are the real legend of Eydis, Bjorn."

"I'm afraid not," he said quietly. "By their own nature, legends are full of inconsistencies and half-truths. There's nothing remotely inconsistent or half-true about my love for you."

"Not all legends are born of lies," Arja whispered. She curled her hand around his neck, laying her head on his heart. "If anyone can live up to his own legend, it's you, Bjorn."

"It's our legend, not just mine," Bjorn corrected her. "I'm no legend without you, *kona*."

"Are you just going to keep arguing with me? Or are you going to kiss me?"

Before he could answer, Arja pulled on Bjorn's tunic, tugging him down to her height as she kissed

THE LEGEND OF EYDIS

him, letting her mouth have the full taste of him as they held onto each other.

As they kissed, Pyri smiled, and Finnar let out a long groan, and Camille, Ephraim, and the other freed sailors talked of home; and beyond them, the clouds overhead parted to shine the sun's light down on the now-empty seas that churned with renewed hope.

THE LEGEND OF EYDIS

THE LEGEND OF EYDIS

C. S. Johnson is the author of several young adult novels, including sci-fi and fantasy adventures including *The Starlight Chronicles* series, the *Once Upon a Princess* saga, and the *Divine Space Pirates* trilogy. With a gift for sarcasm and an apologetic heart, she currently lives in Atlanta with her family.

THE LEGEND OF EYDIS

AUTHOR'S NOTE

Dear Reader,

There are always things that manage to get in the way of a good story.

As with my other work, a lot of different things have gone into this one—some of them surprising, and others completely unexpected. I first had the idea for this book several years ago, which honestly seems longer than it actually is, and this project has been delayed countless times, and a large part of me wonders if this is because so much of it was inspired by my own love story.

It wouldn't be the first time (or probably even the twenty-first time) that my husband has inspired my work. This is the first time that it's an early memory that moves through this work.

While we have been married for ten years now, I still remember the early days of dating and engagement. When we finally did get married—with moonflowers and peacock feathers in my bouquet—we went to Iceland on our honeymoon.

More than ten years later, as I write this, I have never forgotten the fun my husband and I had on those adventures. Chasing down trolls, searching for Christmas elves, watching for the night dragons of the sky (the Aurora Borealis), and climbing up the bell tower of the *Hallgrímskirkja* in Reykjavik ... I have carried and sorted through several of these memories,

THE LEGEND OF EYDIS

piecing them out into my story here in a new way, one that I hope you will allow to add to your pleasure, as much as it's clearly derived from mine.

Though time has passed, Iceland is among my true loves, and I dream of getting to go there again, this time with my own children. I can assure you, I was as desperately in love with my husband when we first went, as much as Bjorn longed for Arja, and I think it's fitting that my love and longing for him have only grown in the last ten years of our lives together. My husband is the true and honorable hero of my heart. I suspect you'll see a similar reoccurring motif in my other work, as I am a willing prisoner to my love for him.

Thank you for spending some more time with me in the world of *The Legend of Eydis*, and as always, dear reader, I hope to see you again soon.

Until We Meet Again,

C. S. Johnson

Thank you for reading! Please leave a review and
check out my other books!

THE LEGEND OF EYDIS